Jane Street

By Kate Kasch

For Mark – this is our year, xoxo

Chapter 1

Her unblinking eyes stare out from under the water - stringy hair floating around a swollen face. She slowly lifts her arms – reaching out with blue-tinged bloated hands. Her blank stare abruptly twists into one of fear – as she's suddenly aware I'm there. She begins to panic. Her arms flail around splashing but her head is stuck under the water, as if being held by some invisible force. I am trying to grab her hands to pull her to safety, but I can't move my body at all. Amidst the chaos I smell something sweet, and then she's mouthing words that have no sound. But I know what she's saying. "Help. Me."

I wake up with a start, disoriented and confused. Sitting up in my bed, I close my eyes and try to slow my breathing. The only sound throughout my hushed apartment is the thumping of my racing heart.

Breathe in.

Breathe out.

Another nightmare.

I glance at the clock, 6:58. Oh no, I'm late!

Ripping my soft down comforter off my sweaty body, I leap out of bed. My room feels abnormally chilly for September in New York City and I shiver as I stumble across the cold wood floors. My heart rate and breath, which were returning to normal – are sprinting once again. Attempting to turn my jumbled brain into some type of coherent thought, I shake my head hard from side to side.

The bathroom tile feels like icicles to my fresh-from-the-warm-bed feet. While simultaneously turning on the shower and peeling off my favorite gray t-shirt with "Albany Law" printed across the front, I get a quick glimpse of myself in the bathroom mirror, and I'm horrified. My skin is even more pale than usual, my large blue eyes are red-rimmed, and my long caramel colored hair is matted to my head in a swirl-like disaster – I'm something straight out of *The Walking Dead.*

Wasting no more time staring at the zombie in the mirror, I quickly finish getting undressed and hop in the shower. With the heat turned up as hot as it will go, the water pours out of the square chrome rainfall shower head. This shower was partly what sold me on this home three years ago, and mornings like these re-confirm my decision. The hot water beats down on my skin and I turn to put my face up into the stream. With my eyes closed, I force myself to relax and focus on the day ahead.

The Board of Directors from the Children's Family Fund (CFF) meet this morning in my office. I am the Director of Development for the charity and responsible for giving an overview of the past year. I will report on the annual fundraising events and how we fared, major donor contributions, the charity's outreach initiatives, our finances as a whole, and most importantly, what's on the horizon. Our biggest news for the year ahead, and what all the Board members really want an update on, is my own special project: an actual home for the children of CFF, being built right here in New York City.

As I get dressed in my slim black Dior suit, jewel-tone purple silk camisole and black leather Louboutin pumps, I go over the meeting agenda in my head. With no time to blow-dry my hair, I put it up damp into a low bun. A quick swipe of mascara, blush and red lipstick – and I'm ready in 25 minutes. Not bad. I'll even have time to stop at Roast to grab myself a large Americano with an extra shot of espresso. Yes, I like my coffee. Strong.

Walking east down West 81st street toward Roast, I take a minute to enjoy this beautiful almost-Fall morning. My tree-lined block with its row of brownstones packed in tightly is still quiet. When I first got a look at this street, I immediately thought: quintessential New York City. My home stands out as one of the few brownstones constructed in a smooth light limestone, including an impressive limestone staircase. Two posts stand proudly at the foot of the stairs, marked with ornate carvings. A grand front door, left in a natural wood tone, awaits the climb, framed by a thick molding. It's the first place I have ever lived that feels like a real home. My friends might argue I don't like to leave it enough.

Once at the coffee shop, the owner greets me with a warm smile as inviting as the aroma in his café. "Good morning, Ms. Townsend. Will it be the usual?"

"Yes please, Frank. Thank you."

I have a seat next to the fireplace while I wait for my coffee. The café is rustic with dark wood and large chandeliers crafted from iron. The focal point of the café is a floor-to-ceiling stone fireplace which boasts a mantel carved from reclaimed wood. It's a little slice of heaven, and reminiscent of my hometown of Albany, within the bustle of the city. Although it's not quite cold enough to warrant a fire this morning, it's still my favorite place to sit and watch the world go by.

With my Americano and a black drip coffee for Evelyn in hand, I grab a cab to midtown. Evelyn Campbell is my boss and the founder of the Children's Family Fund. It's just the two of us in the office on a daily basis, and she and I have grown very close since I started working with her three years ago. CFF is the reason I decided to leave Albany and move to New York City – that and the desire to start fresh where the ghosts from my past could no longer haunt me. Or so I thought.

After getting my bachelor's degree, I was floundering a bit, unsure of what I wanted to do, and where I wanted to go. The feeling that something important awaited me consumed my thoughts and left me frustrated as I struggled with the "what" and the "how." Depending on the universe to guide me, I searched for a sign to point me in the right direction. I got that sign by way of an oncologist at Albany Hospital. My sweet Aunt Marion's diagnosis had me looking to stay local. It was then I decided I would go to Albany Law School.

Aunt Marion raised me since I was 5 years old when my parents died in a horrific car accident. When she grew ill, the grief and loneliness I felt as my only family slipped away devastated me. I think Aunt Marion fought to stay alive long enough to see me graduate from law school, as she passed in hospice care the week of graduation.

Overall, I was a happy law student, enjoying the beautiful campus, the class discussions – even the research, but I can't say I was in love with law the way many of classmates seemed to be. During the summer between my second and third years of law school I interned with the in-house counsel for a non-profit. It was there I found my passion – and it wasn't the law. I finished up my law degree and as my classmates crammed for the Bar Exam, I searched for a position with a non-profit anywhere that wasn't Albany. There was no longer anything there for me but painful memories.

I saw an ad in the *New York Times* for a Director of Development position at a charity which raised funds for orphaned children. The charity was small in comparison to many nationally recognized charities where I assumed I would end up, but the cause spoke to me. After doing my due diligence on the charity's finances and outreach initiatives – I felt excited for the first time in years. I emailed my resume immediately, and I called the charity to introduce myself. I ended up on the phone with Evelyn for over an hour that first phone call. It was like two lost souls had found the balance they each needed in each other. Evelyn confided in me how she and her husband, Mitchell, had tried to have children for years, to no avail. To assuage her grief, Evelyn volunteered to help children who had lost their parents, and through that, found where she belonged. She and Mitchell started the charity soon after, and have been running it themselves for twenty-five years.

Evelyn likes doing all the outreach with the children. Over the years she has created a solid network of people who help her find the children in need, and the couples looking to adopt. She has an innate intuition for matching the children up with the perfect family. Her favorite part of her work is following up with families after an adoption. However, she does not enjoy the business side of running a not-for-profit. That's where I come in. I do the fundraising, which includes pursuing major donors and planning fundraising events. I also do some basic bookkeeping and marketing. We have become a perfect complement to each other.

The same day I had my first phone call with Evelyn, I started looking for town homes in Manhattan. I moved the following week. You can do that when you pay cash.

Chapter 2

Sipping my coffee in the cab ride downtown, my nervous stomach wishes I had grabbed a bite to eat. CFF holds these board meetings twice a year. At this point, I feel very comfortable presenting to the Board, who have all become close business associates and some even friends. But today's meeting is different. It is a smaller group today, just the officers of the Board: president, vice president, treasurer and the charity's attorney. And today the years of work with Realtors, attorneys, mortgage brokers, accountants, and appraisers – never mind all the work raising the capital to fund this project – today is the final meeting where it should all come to fruition. The four officers of the Board of Directors must vote on whether or not to approve the purchase of the building that will become the CFF Home. I am anxious to get this decision made so construction can begin and the first ever CFF Home for Children can be built on Jane Street.

At this point the "signing off" should be a formality, as all four Board officers have put in a lot of work on this project as well. However, I will not be able to relax until I have official approval from the charity's leadership.

Stepping out of the cab at CFF headquarters in Midtown, I glance up the 26 floors of the brick building which has become a second home to me, and my nerves continue to build. It's time. With a deep breath and a sense of determination I stride in through the double doors, across the lobby, into the elevator and up to the 12th floor.

Although I'm in the elevator alone, I can't seem to shake the sensation of another presence with me. The air feels cold and the panicky stabs of claustrophobia threaten my composure – taking me back to last night's nightmare. I take short breaths and rub the back of my neck where my hairs are standing on end. As the elevator makes its climb, I watch each floor number leisurely take its time lighting up. I stare at the glowing digits, willing them to move faster. The silence pounds my ears until finally I feel the elevator stop. As the doors slowly open, I burst out into the hallway gasping for breath.

And I run right into Ryker Rensselaer.

"Verity, are you alright?!" he asks with concern in his eyes.

"Ah, yes. Of course," I answer, slightly embarrassed. "Just anxious for the big meeting. Are you ready with your presentation?"

My tactic to divert attention away from our collision seems to have worked. Ryker flashes me that smile that has even the toughest of women caving to his every whim, and nods his head. "I'm always ready, you know that, Verity."

With a roll of my eyes, we head into my office where Evelyn and the rest of the Board members are waiting. I hand Evelyn her coffee and we exchange a confident look.

I then turn to the group who has assembled around our conference table. They all have their coffees, some glancing at their smart phones, and some chatting quietly with each other. I smile at Mitchell Campbell, Evelyn's husband, and the treasurer of the Board. He is a CPA with Baruch & Co., a large accounting firm in the city. He smiles warmly back at me.

I then scan the rest of the familiar faces. Next to Mitchell sits David Cohen, CFF's attorney, and Mitchell's best friend since childhood. Ryker from Ryker Realty, who is the vice president of the Board, and then Charles "Chip" Watkins, CEO of Toys4Kids, and the president of the Board.

"Hello everyone. Thank you all so much for being here today and for your continued support of CFF. I know you all have busy schedules, so without further ado, I would like to get the meeting started."

Respectfully, all the chatting and email reading stops once I begin speaking. Now with the room's full attention I begin to address the group. By remaining standing, I feel a sense of control as I give an overview of the fundraising efforts from the past year, including what was raised at each event. I also discuss CFF's outreach initiatives, which include the many children whom we have helped get adopted, and scholarships we have given out to deserving children.

After I have run through all my responsibilities I call on Mitch, the treasurer of the Board, to give a financial briefing. Mitch passes out his spreadsheet of all the financials of the charity.

"Due to the aggressive fundraising from the past year, CFF is financially better off than ever. Our working expenses have not changed, and we are in a position to use 90% of our funds raised toward outreach. The charity is only using 10% of the funds raised for working expenses like office rent, supplies, benefits, and salaries. This is an exceptional percentage that few charities in the world can maintain.

Since Verity has asked to receive the smallest salary allowable according to CFF's by-laws, it has really helped us give the maximum amount to those in need. She is truly one-of-a-kind and we feel blessed to have her working with us at CFF."

All the members turn their attention to me and applaud. I offer a nervous smile, but am totally caught off guard by the praise. I know my cheeks are now flushed, and I feel sweat starting to form on my forehead. I subtly wipe my brow. "Thank you, Mitch, that is very kind. But the most important point is the positive financial status the charity has achieved. Due to this financial standing, we have very good news to announce today. So let's move on to the topic we've all been anxious to discuss: Jane Street."

Chapter 3

"With much appreciation to all of you who have helped Evelyn and I realize this dream to create the CFF Home, we are thrilled to announce that, as Mitch has explained, it was a record year for fundraising. We will now be able to buy the building on Jane Street outright, without the need for a loan. This should allow us a faster close on the purchase, followed by an immediate start on the renovations.

At this point I would like you all to hear from Ryker, who can discuss the details of the real estate purchase and the planned renovations. Once Ryker has finished, David will give us an update on the legal paperwork that applies to the deal."

Ryker stands up to address the group. His 6'2" frame offering him a natural advantage in a boardroom. He buttons his blue tailored suit jacket and begins to go through the particulars of the deal.

"As you all know," he begins, "I am a real estate developer, not a broker, but I have asked one of the best real estate agents at my firm to handle this transaction. The appraisers came back with a value that leans in our favor and helped us negotiate a great deal with the owner of the building. On my end, the paperwork is drawn up, all the details have been thoroughly discussed and agreed upon, and the closing is scheduled for this Friday, assuming all goes well today, of course," he says with a smile.

"One thing I would like to discuss with regard to the renovation. The contractor I prefer to use is not available for a start next week. An associate has referred me to another contractor, and although I talked to him a few weeks ago, I have not had the chance to vet him. Verity, I was hoping you could go look at one of his finished projects to approve of his work?"

"Of course," I tell him.

"Great. Thank you. I really don't feel comfortable starting the renovation until we are sure we have the right people in place" Ryker continues.

"David, where are we on the work permit for the construction?" Ryker asks.

"Well, Ryker, as you know -- the architect drew up the plans before we were even under contract on the purchase of the building. And as most of you may know, when renovating in New York City, an expediter is required to file the documents and pull the permits that allow construction projects to move forward. CFF has hired an expediter, my friend, who said they could self-certify those plans which would save us a lot of time. However we may have a setback with the expediter. I'm still working on it," David says a little sheepishly.

"Correct me if I'm wrong" Ryker interjects, "but if your friend, this expediter, can't self certify the architect's plans, then we have to submit the plans and paperwork to the Department of Buildings and wait for approval. Which depending on which plan examiner you get, could be weeks. I thought you had this covered," Ryker says unable to hide his frustration.

"I thought I did too, but I'm not so sure anymore. I'm going to need a little more time," David admits. "I'll work it out.

And once I can get things square with this expediter, then all we need is the contractor to go apply for the permit, which doesn't take long. Usually contractors hire their own expediters to handle that," he adds.

"But that could throw the whole schedule off. I wish you had told me you were having a problem. I might have been able to help," Ryker says as patiently as possible.

"Let's not get worried about something until we know we have to be," I interject. "Why don't we let David work on expediting the permit process while we focus on the purchase and contractor hire."

Ryker and David and the rest of the group agree.

"Great. So I guess we should make this official then: All those in favor of the purchase of 76 Jane Street to be the location of the next CFF Home for Children, say 'aye'." I look around expectantly as all four officers of the Board nod and say 'aye'.

"Without being able to hide my excitement, I allow myself a rare smile.

"Excellent. I can't thank you all enough for your help and guidance. And more importantly, thank you from all the orphaned children who will now have a place to call home." I end the meeting there to avoid letting too much emotion show.

Everyone stands up and shakes hands. It's smiles all around as Ryker, David, Mitchell and Chip congratulate Evelyn and me. Evelyn is glowing with happiness as she skips the handshakes and goes right in for the hugs. It's a beautiful moment as we all realize the years of work are about to produce something so special.

As the members begin to file out of the boardroom, I stop Ryker. "Excuse me, Ryker, would you mind giving me that contractor's information before you go?"

"Always so eager, aren't you Verity," he says with a teasing smile. "God forbid you take a minute to enjoy this major accomplishment. It's right back to business for you."

"Time is precious. I don't like to waste it," I reply.

"Touché," he says as he moves closer to me. In my 4" heels I'm almost able to look him in the eye without straining my neck. I can feel the heat from his body as we stand, almost touching. I know we're getting too close, but I can't quite seem to pull myself away. Almost simultaneously, I hear water splashing and smell that now familiar sickeningly sweet smell. My knees buckle and Ryker catches me by the elbows.

"Whoa. Verity, are you all right? What's happening?" He asks concerned.

Somehow, amidst my haze, I hear Evelyn apologizing for spilling the pitcher of water behind me. I close my eyes, get a good grip on Ryker's forearms, and force my legs to straighten. I slowly open my eyes and I see Ryker's deep blue eyes searching my face for answers.

"I guess I shouldn't have skipped breakfast this morning," I say, trying to lighten the mood.

"But you're shaking, Verity."

"Too much caffeine on an empty stomach. I'm fine. Really." The more I say it, the more I believe it too.

"Haven't you ever heard that breakfast is the most important meal of the day?" Ryker asks lightheartedly.

I can't help but laugh.

"Let me get you that contractor's information so you can go get yourself some pancakes. Oh wait, I mean some healthy green, kale, spinach, protein shake thingy."

"Huh, you know what I eat for breakfast? I didn't know you were paying attention."

"I thought I saw you bring one of those green shakes to a meeting once. Here's the contractor's business card," he says, now desperate to change the subject.

"Thank you. I'll get right on that." And I turn and walk away.

Chapter 4

Back in my office I take a minute to reflect on the morning. I make some notes on the meeting, and start putting together a "to-do" list for the day. As I write down the contractor's number my mind wanders back to Ryker and the strange incident where I thought I might faint. Staring into my computer screen, I slip into a trance-like state.

I'm 6 years old sitting in the guest room at Aunt Marion's house. My fingers toy with the patchwork quilt on the twin bed with the boxy wood frame. Staring out the window into the blackness, I do my best to try and understand it all. The screeching sound of twisting metal, and the smack of the impact - as if someone had taken a cattle prod to our car. When the car crashes to a halt, I sit wide-eyed in the backseat, staring at the bottom of my mommy's favorite brown high heels. Her legs dangle unnaturally on the dashboard, the top half of her body is sprawled on the hood of the car. I want to see her face and ask her if she's okay, but it's too far away. Daddy's head rests on the steering wheel, blood dripping from his forehead and down his ear. His eyes are open and staring – but he can't see me anymore.

I unbuckle my seatbelt and climb out through a small, contorted space, which was once a car window. Sitting on the wet concrete staring up at the pile of metal that was our new blue Lexus sedan, I realize mommy and daddy are no longer here. Two bright balls of light hover over the wreck. They are being summoned up and away, but they won't go. Their presence comforts me and I'm no longer afraid. The soft whisper of my mother's voice is in my ear, she's sorry and I will be okay. They will stay with me in this new form.

When the police and ambulances arrive, I can't answer their questions – they won't understand. Tears stream down my round little cheeks, but no sound escapes my body. For years the only words I speak are to the souls of my parents who visit me in my dreams. I feel a sense of peace and love from them. Although the pull from their next phase in the afterlife must be strong, my parents choose to stay with me for many years, communicating to me through my dreams.

"Verity. Verity, are you okay?" Evelyn now steps into my office, staring at me with deep concern.

Her voice jolts me back to the present. "It's happening again," I say quietly, still staring at my computer.

"What is? What's happening again?" Evelyn asks me, moving closer to my desk.

I shiver a little, and shake off the memory. "Oh. My computer, it's acting up again. I'll just try and re-start it."

"Maybe you should take a little break. Go get something to eat," Evelyn suggests.

"Good idea. I just want to make one phone call, and then I think I'll do that. Thanks, Evelyn."

I make a call to the contractor, Joshua Mesa, and we agree to meet at his newly finished project in Tribeca at 6 p.m. Taking Evelyn's advice, I decide to go get something to eat.

At my favorite organic juice bar, Juice Nation, I order an Orange Kale Protein smoothie, and then, feeling like I need extra fuel, a small raw veggie wrap. With my lunch in hand, I walk outside to what has turned out to be a beautiful day in the city. Fall is my absolute favorite time of year in New York, and I decide to eat my lunch outside. Spying an open table at Bryant Park, I sit and eat my lunch, and lose myself watching the throngs of people rushing past.

Back at the office, I spend a few hours going over the CFF Home's design ideas with the architect and interior designer, and begin planning the early stages of the launch party event for the Home. This part of the job is so enjoyable to me. The freedom to create a space and an atmosphere that can transport people out of their normal lives and into the world I invent, inspires me. Keeping to a strict budget can be difficult, but my negotiating class at Albany Law taught me that the first contract you receive is just a suggestion -- always ask for more. I guess law school wasn't a total waste of time.

In researching the contractor, Joshua Mesa, I don't turn up any bad reviews, which is a good start. His website is simple, but effective. He has before and after photos from finished projects and I choose a few and skim through the homes and offices (mostly homes) completely furnished down to the drapes. There are bowls of fruit on the counters, the dining room tables are completely set with china, candles are lit in the bathrooms, and beautiful art hangs on the walls. I knew Mr. Mesa must be talented in order for Ryker to even consider him, and I'm impressed already.

At 5:15 p.m. I peek my head into Evelyn's office where she sits staring at her computer screen.

"Evelyn, I'm going to head down to Tribeca to meet with the contractor now. You should go home – you look exhausted!"

"Ok, dear. And you're right – it has been a long day, hasn't it? I'm just worried about that permit situation with David. If he doesn't come through for us, it will really set our timeline back in a major way," she says with a furrowed brow.

"There's nothing we can do about that tonight. So please don't worry so much. Hopefully this contractor is reliable, hardworking and talented – and maybe he will have his own solution for the permit. We will figure it out. We always do," I reassure her.

That makes Evelyn smile. I see her quickly reminisce about the last 3 years and all the "impossible" things we have accomplished.

"Well, I'm sure you're right, as usual," she says looking relieved.

"I can even call you after I meet with Mr. Mesa later, if that will ease your mind."

"That would be wonderful, Verity. Thank you. And I think I will join you on your way out. You are right - I'm exhausted. My slippers and a glass of wine are calling to me."

We take the elevator down to the lobby. Out on the street I hail a cab for Evelyn, see her into the car and wave good-bye as the car makes its way to the Upper East Side where the Campbell's live.

I then have to wait, what seems like forever, before seeing another available cab. It is rush hour in the city – and I am not exactly known for my patience. I try the Uber app on my phone and the wait is 10 minutes. This makes me once again consider getting a driver. However, the idea of having my own driver seems a little embarrassing. But, I wouldn't be standing on 44th street with my hand raised for 15 minutes!

Once in the cab I give the driver the address in Tribeca. I look at my watch, 5:40 – whew, just going to make it, barring any traffic disaster. I take the 20-minute ride downtown to go over the questions I want to ask Mr. Mesa. However, I know the before and after result of his most recently finished project will speak for itself. The apartment he just completed is a residential building, and although we'll be doing something more on the commercial side, I think it should still be a valid gauge of his work.

The cab pulls in front of the Tribeca Park building on Chambers Street a few minutes before 6 p.m. Before heading in, I take a moment to assess the building. It's an impressive waterfront building with a cobblestone entryway and giant columns. As I head in through the double doors, I take note of the beautifully designed foyer. At the front desk, I give my name and explain I am meeting Joshua Mesa on the sixth floor.

The doorman calls up to Mr. Mesa and points me in the direction of the elevators. Alone in the elevator a strange chill takes over my body. The air is thick with that nauseating sweet smell again and I begin to gasp for breath. I grab on to the wall of the elevator, afraid for the second time that day I might collapse. There seems to be no air left in the small cube. Just when I think I can't take it anymore, there is a "ding" and the elevator door opens. Still holding on for support I make it out into the hallway. I lean against the wall to catch my breath.

After giving myself a few minutes to regain composure, I walk to the door of the apartment. Angry with myself for being late, I shake it off and ring the bell.

Joshua Mesa is about six feet tall with salt and pepper hair kept a little shaggy. He has a short scruffy beard that is somewhere between "I haven't shaved in 3 days" and "this beard is intentionally not trying too hard." It suits him. He wears a blue and gray flannel shirt with the sleeves rolled up, a pair of broken-in jeans and boots. His small, serious brown eyes are sharp and clear. He doesn't miss a thing. I can appreciate that.

I extend my hand with a smile, "Mr. Mesa, I'm Verity Townsend from the Children's Family Fund."

"Of course, Verity. So nice to meet you. Come on in, and please, call me Josh." I follow Josh through the foyer and into the kitchen.

"Verity. That's an interesting name. Any special meaning behind it or were your parents just hippies like mine?" Josh says with a smile.

"It actually means "truth." My mother was into gematria, numerology, horoscopes, the paranormal . . . so yes, total hippie."

"Truth, huh" Josh said. "I'm assuming that means you will be totally honest about how you feel about my work. No holds barred type thing?"

"You would be correct. Sugar-coating does not exist in my vocabulary."

"Well, then I guess I'll know right where I stand. I like that," Josh says in a discerning tone.

Josh takes out an iPad and shows me photos of the apartment before it was renovated. There were walls everywhere separating a lot of smaller rooms. It is quite a contrast to see the large open spaces now bringing in natural light from all angles.

As we walk around the apartment I continue to check back at the "before" photos, almost in disbelief that it is the same space. The kitchen is in a totally different location and now opens up into the main living room. There are new hardwood floors throughout the apartment. There is a breakfast bar with marble countertops, and white cabinets. The appliances are disguised with cabinet fronts, creating a cohesive, bright area that is definitely a place I would like to cook in. A neutral palette finishes off the living and dining rooms. Textured wallpaper and accents in shades of white, cream and gray add dimension. I peek my head into each of the two bedrooms, which are done in a similar color scheme with appropriate pops of color for interest. Overall the feel of the apartment is luxurious, yet comfortable. It's exactly what I'm looking for.

"Each bedroom has an en suite bathroom attached, would you like to see those as well?"

"I think I've seen enough," I tell him.

"Well, what do you think? You've been pretty quiet this whole time. It's tough to know what you're thinking. And I've got to say, it's a little unnerving."

"The whole apartment is beautiful. You have really done a spectacular job transforming the space. I can see you have quite an eye for detail. The layout, design and craftsmanship are excellent. I do have a few questions."

Josh visibly relaxes, "Whew, that's a relief. I'm going to be honest with you, my business is still on the smaller side, and getting a job that's connected to Ryker Realty could really help take things to the next level."

"I can understand that. And if your work is as good as I think it is, I'm sure this can be a very successful partnership. Do you have up-to-date insurance on file?"

"Yes, I do. I am licensed and have up-to-date insurance," Josh answers.

"Excellent. And how long does it typically take you to obtain a work permit? Do you go to the D.O.B. yourself, or do you have an expediter do that for you?"

"Well I used to go by myself, but now I have an expediter do it and I get it approved much quicker. I can sometimes get it approved in a day with my guy. He's amazing. Why, are you having a problem with the process?"

"Well, I'm not sure yet. But that is comforting to know that you'll be ready to go once we close. And I'm curious – who does your carpentry? These cabinets look custom made."

"They are custom. My brother, Johnny, is a very talented carpenter. He does the custom carpentry work on all my projects. We're a good team." Josh says with pride.

"Are you two interior decorators as well? I mean the décor is just perfect."

"We have an interior designer that comes and stages our residential projects. I was unsure about paying for staging, but after the first time I tried it, the reaction from potential buyers was unreal. After that I was convinced. It's worth every penny."

"I'm convinced too!" I say with a smile. "I have confidence in you and your team. I think you would be a perfect fit to turn Jane Street into a comfortable home for orphaned children. Are you available at the beginning of next week?" I ask.

Josh can't hide his enthusiasm. "I'm finished with this project, and ready for 76 Jane Street!"

"Great! I will be in touch tomorrow for definite times. Let's tentatively schedule to meet at Jane Street on Monday at 9 a.m. to do a walk-through and discuss the architect's plans," I say pulling out my iPhone to access my calendar.

"That sounds perfect. Thank you for the opportunity, Verity. I won't disappoint you."

"You're welcome. And I look forward to working with you and your team." I put my hand out and Josh encloses his hands around it. We stand there for a moment, eyes locked on each other. After realizing it's been an unusually long time for a handshake, I pull my hand away and start to make my way to the front door, a little flustered.

"Have a good night, Josh"

Chapter 5

Out in the hallway I see the elevator in front of me, and thinking I'm losing my mind, I decide to take the stairs. It's only six flights - the exercise will be good for me.

As I walk out of the double lobby doors into the crisp fall air, for the second time that day I wish I had a driver. I settle for hailing a cab, which doesn't take too long since Tribeca is not as frantic as Midtown, and it's a little later in the evening.

The cab drops me off outside my townhouse, and as I begin to climb the ten or so stairs up to my front door, I realize how exhausted I am. It has been a long day. All I can think of doing is cozying up on my couch with a glass of cabernet.

I unlock the heavy front door, step inside, and place my handbag and keys on the small table in the foyer. Shivering, I immediately walk to the thermostat and turn the heat up. The track lights that line the exposed wood beams along the ceiling in the kitchen illuminate the room. With a generous glass of Caymus in hand and Mumford & Sons playing softly through the surround sound, I plop down on the couch in the attached living room. My eyes close, and sleep feels but a minute away, until I hear a rumble in my stomach. Food trumps sleep.

The doublewide Viking refrigerator, fit for a large family, looks almost empty with the few things I need in it. After surveying the inventory, I decide on a veggie wrap. I slice up cucumbers, tomato and fresh mozzarella, add some hummus and wrap it all up in a whole-wheat tortilla. Sitting at the kitchen island, which seats six, I eat my wrap while reading the newspaper on my iPad. Nothing turns the brain off more than the gossip on *Page Six* of the *NY Post.*

Upstairs after dinner, with one square of dark chocolate and my wine, I quickly change out of my suit and into my flannel pajamas. The chill I felt since I got home just won't seem to melt away, not even with wine and flannel. Snuggled under my duvet, I put HGTV on my television, and I'm asleep in five minutes.

It's quiet and dark but I see a dull light in the distance. There is a calming smell and I am relaxed and feel weightless. I lay back and close my eyes, floating. Suddenly a strong force pushes on my shoulders – my eyes snap open, alarmed. I'm in water and someone or something is holding me under. I can't see them but I can feel the pressure on my upper body. I struggle to grab at them, to get my face above the water. I just need air. I'm gasping for breath as water fills my lungs. Panic sets in as I realize - this is the end . . .

Filled with fear and dismay, I sit up abruptly, sucking in air. I'm okay, I keep repeating to myself. It was a dream. It was a nightmare. I lay back down with a deep breath and stare at my ceiling, calming down. The television is still on HGTV from last night, and this early in the morning an infomercial drones on – three women with too much makeup are hawking some imitation diamond bracelets. It's all too normal for the way I feel right now.

After the car accident, along with the dreams where I could communicate with my parents after their death, I also had traumatic nightmares. Nightmares where I would relive the car crash, or be the victim in a horrible home invasion were common. Sometimes my nights were filled with intense feelings of abandonment and loneliness. And then it got worse – with Jessica Jones.

I had a dream about Jessica Jones, a girl in my second grade class. In the dream Jessica was lost in the woods – I could feel her panicked fear, and she was so, so cold. My body would not warm up the entire week Jessica was missing. In my dreams, I kept seeing a big tree that had an old tree stand on it, like the ones that hunters would use. After Jessica had been missing for a few days, the community organized a search party. Aunt Marion and I, along with many families from my school, participated in the search for Jessica. Two days went by and there was no sign of her. At that time, I still had not spoken since my parents' accident. As our boots crunched through the snow covered woods in the search line, with Aunt Marion on one side of me, and Sheriff Lamm on the other, I turned to the Sheriff and uttered my first words in years: "Tree stand. She's at the tree stand."

Jessica's shrunken body was huddled at the base of a large tree. Steel climbing sticks dotted their way up the tall trunk, leading to an old wooden tree stand high up in the branches. As other members of the search party sobbed around me, I stared at Jessica's frozen little body, looking for the white ball of light above it. I soon realized, that light was long gone. Only the body her soul inhabited was left behind for her family to bury and mourn.

These dreams, or visions, happened throughout my childhood until I found a way to block them out. Immersing myself in someone else's pain, fear, suffering, was too much for me to bear. And now, I'm afraid it's happening again. For some unknown reason, it seems the spirit of a dead woman has sought me out as a vessel with whom to communicate. I need to find out who she is and why she chose me. Having now felt her horror of being drowned, murdered, I will not stop until this poor woman's soul has found peace.

The clock shows 5:30 a.m. – there's no point in trying to go back to sleep. I need to run – to hit the pavement and let me body feel alive – to get my heart rate up in a positive way.

Slowly rolling out of my bed, I trudge over to my dresser and grab my black full length running leggings, and a long sleeve Under Armour reflective top – it's dark out there. With my hair in a high ponytail, and my headphones in my hand, I go to disarm the security system, and much to my surprise, it is already disarmed. Did I forget to set the alarm when I came in last night? I was really tired but setting the alarm for me is habitual.

Flustered and frustrated with myself, I pull open the front door and the cold air hits me like a slap in the face. A light layer of frost makes the sidewalk and street gleam under the glow of the streetlights. It must be the first frost, I think with a shiver. As I take a minute to stretch on the sidewalk, I can't stop thinking about the nightmare and the security system. My solution: Meghan Trainor. With the music pumping, I'm off on a run, not a jog, a run. There's a difference.

My body feels a bit heavy to start, but after about a mile it warms up and I find my groove and get lost in the rhythm. With each step I work on pushing the nightmare out of my head and half way through the 5 mile run, it works. I love running the streets of New York before the city is fully awake. By the time I arrive back at my townhouse, I feel great. I have planned out my day at work and I'm focused and alert.

It's early when I arrive to work, so after leaving Evelyn's coffee in her office, I take a moment to relax at my desk. Sipping my coffee, I admire my little view of bustling Midtown Manhattan. When I first started at CFF, the office was, well, depressing. One of my first orders of business as Director of Development was to re-decorate. Initially, Evelyn showed some resistance to the changes, however, once I explained that you can't bring major donors into this dark and dated office to try and woo them, she warmed to the idea. And then I told her I'd pay for it, and she was sold.

The main door to CFF opens up into a small sitting area. Off that room there are two offices, Evelyn's and mine. A decent sized conference room with a table that seats ten, a kitchenette area and a bathroom round out the space. A little paint and new furniture goes a long way. With my office, I put in an L shaped desk that allows me to look out the window as well as face the door when I want to. My favorite change was the addition of artwork created by the children of CFF. I had pieces of the children's artwork framed and hung in the sitting room and both offices. Evelyn was brought to tears by this detail, and told me she felt so much positive energy in the office now. I couldn't agree more. The space is now peaceful, comfortable and inspiring.

The click of my office door handle disrupts the silence of my office. I turn around ready to greet Evelyn, but no one is there. The door is open about 8 inches, which is strange because it's a heavy door with a long handle that needs to be pulled all the way down for the door to open. I feel the air around me get cold and goose bumps form on my arms. There is an overwhelming sadness that permeates my office and I close my eyes to try and understand. And then I hear a voice, "Verity?"

Startled, I open my eyes. Now, Evelyn is standing by my office door looking at me concerned. "Are you okay? You look so . . . Sad. Did something happen?"

Almost immediately the cold air and heaviness that surrounded me is gone. I smile at Evelyn, "I'm fine." I reassure her. "Just didn't have a great night's sleep."

"The nightmares are back?" She asks quietly.

I look down at my hands "Yes. They are. They are a little different this time, though." More terrifying, I think to myself. "But I'm fine. Really. Your coffee is in your office on your desk," I add, changing the subject.

Evelyn pauses to look at me a second longer, and then decides to let me off the hook.

"Oh, thank you, Verity. It's so thoughtful of you to always remember my coffee. But, what you did not remember . . . to call me last night after your meeting with the contractor," she raises an eyebrow in a mock scolding way.

"Oh my. I am so sorry! I completely forgot. I guess I'm a little distracted lately . . ." I trail off.

"Well, tell me some good news. Please!"

Always elegant, today Evelyn is dressed in a knee length olive green skirt, cream silk blouse, light brown sheer tights (she calls them "stockings"), and brown kitten heel pumps. Her dark brown hair is tied up in her signature French twist. And she has on a full face of make-up. And by that, I mean a *lot* of make-up. I have often thought that since Evelyn is nearing 70, maybe she can't quite see how much makeup she is actually putting on? I'm not sure – but now I can't picture her any other way.

I have never once seen Evelyn wear pants to work. She says she finds it unprofessional for an executive director. Even amidst the snowy winter days in New York City, Evelyn is one of very few New Yorkers in a skirt. They just don't make them like her anymore.

"I have great news. Mr. Mesa seems very capable. He is professional, has an incredible eye for detail, a great team around him, and is very eager to impress us, and in turn, impress Ryker. That will definitely work in our favor. And perhaps, best of all, he is licensed, his insurance is up-to-date and he has some miracle expediter that can get work permits in a day! I have asked him to meet us on Monday at Jane Street – since at that point the building will be ours!"

"Oh, that is great news! Sometimes it's hard to believe this is actually going to happen. It has been such a long time coming."

"I know what you mean," I say as we both take a moment to think back over the years.

'Well" Evelyn says, "My coffee is calling me -- I think I'll go check my email and get the day started."

"Of course. One quick thing before you go -- when you arrived this morning, was my office door open?" I ask her.

"Actually, yes, it was. I remember being surprised since you always keep it closed." A troubled expression crosses my face. "Is everything alright, Verity?" Evelyn asks, her green eyes showing concern.

"Of course it is, Evelyn – please, don't worry about a thing."

"Ok. Just keep me apprised of the Jane Street progress, and please follow up with David regarding the permit." With that, Evelyn leaves my office to head to hers, closing the door with a "click" as she exits.

Chapter 6

I leave Roast at 8:40 a.m. on Friday morning with five coffees in a cardboard drink holder – Evelyn's, Mitchell's, Chip's, David Cohen's, and mine. The cab arrives at the offices of Hancock, Metz and Cohen, the attorney's office where the Jane Street real estate closing will take place, with minutes to spare. Exiting the cab while balancing the coffees in the holder is like a circus act. Four of the cups are pushed in and secure in the holder, but the fifth cup sits precariously in the middle of the four, a little wobbly. I am so focused on my coffees, I almost smack right into a tall man on the street in a long navy topcoat.

"Oh, excuse me," I say looking up, right into the deep blue eyes of Ryker Rensselaer.

"I'm starting to think you're knocking into me on purpose, Verity," Ryker says with that devil of a smile.

"Ha. Funny. But seriously, what are you doing here?" I ask him.

"You didn't think I'd miss this monumental occasion, did you? I'm here for the closing, of course. Is one of those coffees for me?"

"Wow. Thanks Ryker. I really appreciate it. And I know it will ease Evelyn's mind having the extra support here as well. She was so nervous yesterday! Unfortunately, since I had no idea you'd be here, I did not get you a coffee."

"No problem. Let's just say you owe me one," Ryker says as he moves to open the door for me.

"I wouldn't go that far," I shoot back at him. He feigns surprise and disappointment.

We ride the elevator up to the law office, and I hate to admit to myself how happy I am to have Ryker by my side. Since my last two experiences in elevators have been less than pleasant, I had been dreading the ride since I woke up this morning. We arrive on the 22nd floor with no incident (cue my deep sigh of relief.)

Once in the lobby we see the Board members already there. Evelyn, Mitchell, Chip and David are talking quietly amongst themselves – and all chatter seems to stop when we enter, as everyone turns to look at Ryker and me. Oh no, they think we came together.

"Look who I bumped into on the street!" I announce.

"Oh Ryker, how thoughtful of you!" Evelyn says as she goes in for a hug.

"Evelyn, I wouldn't think of missing this," Ryker says with a smile that has Evelyn swooning.

"Oohhh Verity, please tell me one of those coffees is for me," says Chip, who despite the cooler fall weather and more formal setting is always dressed like he's on a resort vacation, including the tan. Today he is wearing a pale pink button down and light khaki cotton pants. "You know me, mornings are not my thing."

"It sure is, Chip. Yours is right here," I say as I pass him a coffee. I then hand out the rest and finally get to take a sip of mine, which is thankfully still warm.

David thanks me for his coffee and then explains, "Well, we certainly do have quite the crew here today. Thank you all for coming. However, I'm afraid it will only be me, Evelyn and Mitchell allowed in the office for the closing. We don't want to scare our seller away now, right? Verity, Chip and Ryker you three will have to wait out here in the lobby."

"Of course, David. And could we grab a quick word after the closing?" I ask him.

Just then one of David's assistants calls the group in, and David scoots through the doorway. Is he avoiding me?

Chip, Ryker and I have a seat on the plush chairs in the lobby. The furnishings are comfortable, yet sophisticated, with beautiful colorful artwork lining the walls. Along with a selection of magazines on the coffee table, there are fresh flowers in a low crystal vase. The lamps on the side tables are a pot shaped hammered bronze base with a cream linen shade. Very nicely done.

"So Chip, what's the new 'it' toy for the holidays this year?" I ask him. Chip is the CEO of Toys4Kids, a family owned toy company that has been around for decades.

I immediately see his face light up as he starts to explain some toy that helps young children learn to code phone apps – and I seriously can't believe how far toys have come since the simple blocks and dolls I played with as a child.

I have always thought of Chip as a kid at heart, and his passion for his work is evident as he goes on about some new toys his R&D department is coming out with. It is pretty fascinating.

Before we know it, the door to David's office is opening and I see Evelyn emerging with a giant smile on her face. Today she is wearing a black wool knee length skirt with a wine colored silk blouse that has pearl buttons down the back. She looks beautiful as her eyes dance with excitement. She heads straight over to me and wraps her arms around me in a warm embrace.

Not typically comfortable with this kind of affection, today I decide to relax and let it happen. She did just write a check for millions of dollars to buy a building that I convinced her was necessary. The least I could do is give her a hug.

"Now, your first order of business with Jane Street," Evelyn says as she pulls out of the hug. "Make copies of this!" Evelyn holds up a small bronze key with the number 76 on it.

"Wow – this really makes it official. So exciting! Is that the only key?" I ask.

"Yes, as you know it was previously a garage for another building before the owner turned it into a home. Since he was single, he only had one key made. We'll want to make a few for you, me, a spare, the contractor, and whoever else might need/want one. But first, why don't we go celebrate the purchase of the future home for CFF's children!"

"Can I join you two lovely ladies?" Ryker asks. "Why don't we have lunch down in the Village – your soon-to-be new neighborhood."

"Of course!" Evelyn says a little too eagerly, in my opinion. "I never turn down a meal with a successful, handsome man. We would love the company, right Verity?"

I just smile and nod.

Down in Greenwich Village, over a lunch of fresh spinach salads and warm soups, the three of us talk excitedly about Jane Street. I suggest that Evelyn and I meet down at the building tomorrow morning for the first official walk-through as the owners of the building.

"Oh that's a great idea, Verity! Ryker, please join us. It was never completely finished and can be a little spooky, if you ask me. We would love a big strapping man to escort us. It's a Saturday morning, so you should have time, right?" Evelyn says while smiling at Ryker.

Big strapping man. Seriously? What is this, the 1950s?

"That sounds like an excellent idea, Evelyn. I would be honored to join you two."

After a trip to the locksmith to have four new keys made, I then arranged for a bike messenger to deliver keys to Josh, Ryker and David - keeping two at the office for Evelyn and me. I leave a message with David regarding the permit issue. In all the excitement after the closing, I forgot to ask him about it. I also spoke with Josh about meeting on Monday at Jane Street to discuss the architect's plans, and do an overall walk-through. Josh's excitement was clear as we spoke on the phone.

Arriving home that evening, I just want to snuggle in my bed with a glass of wine and a funny movie. I walk up the steps to my front door and take my keys out of my handbag, accidentally dropping my keys in the process. As I reach down to grab them, my elbow pushes against the door and the door creaks open.

How is that possible? I absolutely remember locking the door and setting the alarm when I left this morning. Cautiously stepping inside into my foyer, I lock the door behind me and set the alarm. Walking through the main level of my house cautiously, my mind is racing. There has to be a logical explanation for this. Who else has a key to my house? My cleaning lady, Grace, is the only one with a key. Wait, Friday is Grace's day to clean – she must have forgotten to lock the door. I immediately call her and using all my restraint to keep my voice from shaking, I ask Grace about the door.

"Ms. Verity, I know I locked the door. I definitely remember setting the alarm and locking the door. I've been with you for three years and I have never forgotten this." She says in her Portuguese accented English.

"The door was open when I got home, and no one else has a key, Grace."

"Well it wasn't me," Grace says stubbornly.

Ugh, I give up. I once again remind Grace the importance of locking up before she leaves, and then I hang up the phone. I'm even more exhausted than I was 20 minutes ago. I head straight for the wine.

As I pour myself a glass of cabernet, I decide my weekend is going to be filled with exercise and sleep. At that moment my phone rings, and I look at the screen and see my best friend, Tessa's, smiling face.

"Hi Tessa!" I answer, trying to sound upbeat.

"Verity! You actually answered – it's a miracle!" Tessa says in her high-pitched voice.

I can just picture her blonde hair – all wild and curly. And although her freckles have faded over the years, I still see her as a giggly nine-year-old covered in them.

"What are you talking about – when it's you, I always answer. Well more than for anyone else at least."

"I guess I can't ask for any more than that," she says. "So, I have a feeling you desperately need a night out with your best friend since grade school," she says. And I can feel the smile in her voice.

"Ugh Tessa – I don't know. I'm exhausted. It was a crazy week. What makes you think I *need* a night out, anyway?"

"You pretty much always need a night out. You are the only single 28 year old in New York City who never goes out. And I'm dying to check out this new DJ – you have to come with me. *Pleeeeease?*"

"How do I say no to that?" I laugh.

"You don't. You say yes." Tessa says confidently. She has me convinced, and she knows it. "Ok, so I'm going to come to your place tomorrow night around 7:30 so that I can raid your closet, and your wine cellar. And then we will head out from there! See you tomorrow!" And she hangs up before I can get a word in - so much for my quiet weekend at home.

Although no specific nightmare, my sleep is plagued with terrifying screams, the feelings of confusion and panic, and that thick, sweet smell that chokes my throat. After tossing and turning most of the night I wake up on Saturday morning sweaty and cranky. I definitely do not feel like going out tonight. Dragging myself out of bed, I skip the coffee and go directly into the bathroom and take a long, hot shower.

Chapter 7

One positive reason to have Ryker along for the first official walk-through of the CFF Home —he has a car service. It was pretty luxurious to have a car waiting right outside my townhouse – ready to whisk the three of us down to Greenwich Village.

Once we arrive at Jane Street, Evelyn heads up the few stairs to the front door, and begins to mess with the key. I spend a minute on the sidewalk taking it all in. The short little block with its cobblestone street and low-rise brick buildings. Small trees line both sides of the street. The red brick townhomes have front stoops with wrought iron railings and flowerpots overflowing with mums. The building that will soon be the CFF Home is a brick townhouse three stories high on the north side of the street between Greenwich and Washington Streets. Although it's relatively new compared to the rest of the block, the previous owner did a great job of creating a building that blends in with the rest of the town homes on the street.

Lost in thought, I don't notice Ryker has joined me on the sidewalk. He follows my gaze up the building. "It seems like the previous owner really cared about having his home match the historical integrity of the rest of the homes on the block," Ryker says.

"I was just thinking that same thing," I say as I turn to him. "You would never think this building was built in the last five years. But I do wonder why the owner never finished it."

"Usually in situations like this, work stops because the person runs out of money. Poor guy. Unfortunately I see this kind of thing all the time."

"You mean, you benefit from this kind of thing all the time. Don't you swoop in and buy real estate at a steep discount when owners are desperate to sell?" I challenge him.

"First of all, it's all about perspective. The way I see it, I am helping these people dig themselves out of whatever hole they're in. Trust me, most of these people are relieved to shed the weight of a mortgage they can no longer afford," Ryker explains. "And secondly, at this point, I am not buying from individuals – it's mostly larger companies in financial distress."

"Well, I guess that's one way to look at it. If that helps you sleep at night," I tease him.

"Ouch, Verity. Right between the eyes – that's your style, huh?" Ryker says looking wounded.

Feeling contrite, I change the subject. "So this street has a fascinating history, do you know anything about it? You are the king of New York real estate, right?"

"You are correct on both counts. I am, in fact, the king of New York real estate; and I do know the history of this street. 80 Jane Street, right there across the street," he says pointing to a brick town home on the south side of the street. "That building is an historical landmark. It is the location where Alexander Hamilton actually died. After the famous duel in Weehawken, NJ where Aaron Burr shot Hamilton, Dr. Hosack, the doctor that accompanied Hamilton to the duel, brought him here to 80-82 Jane Street, the Bayard mansion. It was the home of Hamilton's best friend, William Bayard. A large bedroom on the second floor of the mansion was prepared for Hamilton. He lasted a little more than a day before he passed away. The Bayard family was said to have never cleaned up Hamilton's blood that soaked into the floor – to honor their fallen hero."

"Wow, you do know a lot about this," I say, surprised. I try to picture the street back in the early 1800's with dirt roads and big fields.

"I am completely fascinated with Alexander Hamilton. I have done a lot of research on him," Ryker says.

"So I'm assuming you went to see the Broadway show, *Hamilton,* then?" I ask.

"I've seen it three times already," Ryker says a little shyly. " I had been studying up on Hamilton before the show came out, and you can't even understand how excited I was when I heard about a show about Hamilton's life coming to Broadway. You could say I'm a superfan."

"You are full of surprises, Mr. Rensellear." A light fall breeze blows the crispy leaves scraping along the sidewalk, and I rub my arms to warm myself from the chill. I look over at Ryker and our eyes lock on each other with a palpable intensity.

Ryker looks like he's about to say something when we are suddenly interrupted by Evelyn's voice yelling down to us, "I finally got this darn key to work. Let's go on in!"

As we walk into the house and close the front door to the outside noise, the emptiness echoes. It's cool and dark and dusty inside, but I can hardly contain my excitement. From the moment I first stepped foot in this building a few months ago, I knew I had found what I was looking for. It felt like home. I could immediately picture the sitting area by the front door. The raw wood staircase to the left of the front foyer, had the potential to be grand, once re-finished. The color palette would be different than the subdued neutrals in the CFF Office. The main living room, which is the first room to the right in the front of the house, will have slate gray walls, turquoise couches and lime green pillows. I also picture turning the formal living room, in the rear of the house, into a room filled with wall to wall desks where the children could study – with a rainbow striped wall and brightly colored desk chairs. I think I might enjoy decorating this place more than I did my own home. With a kid-centric design, there are no boundaries. It's going to be a blast.

As I'm pointing out the new design layout to Ryker, he interrupts me, "I meant to ask you - how did things go with the contractor, Mr. Mesa?"

"I'm so sorry for not following up with you," I apologize. "We had a great meeting, his latest project was fabulous, and he sure seemed excited to be working on a project you are connected to. Talk about superfan – I think you have one in Josh," I say with a laugh.

"Oh really? I like him already. So 'Josh', huh? You two are already on a first name basis? That's fast for you, isn't it Verity?"

"Oh wow, Ryker. Jealousy does not look good on you."

"I thought everything looked good on me," Ryker says all too seriously.

I roll my eyes.

"Let's head to the back to the kitchen. It is the heart of the home after all!" Evelyn interjects in an attempt to cut the tension.

We open the door and step into the kitchen. The temperature seems to drop 20 degrees, as the wind whistles through the windows. The entire atmosphere has changed. I am almost overwhelmed by grief and sorrow. I steady myself by grabbing onto the countertop. I need to sit down.

Just then, the door slams shut behind us and we all jump.

"This wind is unreal," says Evelyn, a little shaken. "And I guess we're going to have to do something about the insulation in here - it's chilly isn't it?!" She says with a nervous chuckle.

I am now fully leaning against the counter, trying to keep from collapsing. My legs don't seem to want to work. The wind whistles once more and the whole back of the building shakes. The whining of the wind starts to sound more like a moan to me - its human sound echoing through the empty kitchen and into the depths of my brain. I need to get out of here.

As if reading my mind, Evelyn says, "I'm freezing and this wind is so loud! Why don't we head out and grab a bite to eat – I'm famished." Although we didn't make it through the upstairs, it's pretty clear we all want out of this building.

"That sounds lovely, Evelyn," Ryker agrees. I am still unable to speak. Ryker offers me his arm and I gratefully accept it. Somehow, I shakily walk out of Jane Street leaning on Ryker for support. Although I'm sure he can feel and see my delicate state, he says nothing. I am so thankful; I vow to stop giving him such a hard time. Well, maybe just through lunch.

Chapter 8

I spend the rest of my Saturday going for a run, and doing some errands. After a quick pop into my local health food store, I then stop into my neighborhood florist to fill my apartment with cheery fall floral arrangements. I bring home bunches of chrysanthemums in reds, oranges and yellows. The whole aura of my apartment seems dark and sad lately, I definitely need to change the atmosphere and brighten things up. Hopefully the happy flowers will do the trick.

Before I know it, it's 7:15 and I hear a knock at my door. Only Tessa would be early - always anxious to get things started. I open the door and there's Tessa standing on my stoop –wild curls and wide smile. I'm immediately in a better mood. She has that effect on me. Well, she has that effect on most people.

"V!" Tessa squeals as she wraps me in a giant hug.

"Hey Tess – I see you're early, as usual," I'm teasing her, but I'm also smiling.

"Well, the earlier I get here, the earlier we can get the party started! Now pour me a glass of wine and turn up the music," she says as she charges to the back of the house and into the kitchen. "I brought us some nibbles since I know the one thing you never have here is real food."

"That's not true! I picked up some hummus, veggies and rice crackers today. They are a perfect accompaniment to wine."

"As I said, you never have any real food here. But no worries, I brought bread, meats, cheeses and olives – lots of good stuff. You can eat your veggies and rice crackers. Now, pour me a glass of wine."

"You sure are demanding. How does a Malbec sound? I can open this one?" I hold up a bottle.

"That looks perfect. I completely trust your taste in wine." Tessa scrolls through my iPad to change the music.

With the wine poured and the music pumping through the surround sound speakers, Tessa and I talk and laugh for a while in the kitchen. We get so caught up in our conversation that before we know it, an hour has passed.

"Oh my goodness – it's 8:30! We need to get dressed!" Tessa exclaims.

"Oh, right! Are you sure you don't want to just hang out here tonight?" I ask hopefully.

"Absolutely not." Tessa says. "You need to get out of this house! And I do too. It will be fun, I promise! Now, up to THE closet," she says, with a sparkle in her eyes.

I understand why Tessa is excited about my closet. Over the past 3 years, I have nurtured a rather (un)healthy obsession with shopping. Growing up, although I never went without, I also didn't have a lot. Designer clothes were nowhere on my radar. I was the tall, awkward girl, wearing generic sneakers and leggings from Target. I wasn't shy, but I was reserved. I let very few people into my world. Tessa was the opposite end of the spectrum. Pint-sized and spunky, her personality and openness was magnetic. She could throw on an oversized t-shirt with cut-off jeans, and look fabulous. Most likely, the following day, you would see ten other girls in over-sized t-shirts and cut-off jeans. Tessa could make a mundane school day seem like a magical adventure. I always told her she should have her own reality show.

The two of us may have appeared to be an odd pairing, but the saying 'opposites attract' exists for a reason. In Tessa, I found light and warmth, and an encouraging word to try something new or give someone a chance.

In me, Tessa found someone that didn't expect her to be "on" all the time. She didn't need to make fireworks out of chalk dust for me to like her. I am a good listener, and I have always taken her thoughts and ideas seriously. That's why in eighth grade when Tessa told me she would move to New York City after high school to work in art, I believed her. And although her 13 year-old self didn't quite know what it meant to "work in art," she did just what she said. New York City has never been the same.

On my 21st birthday, my Aunt Marion told me about a trust my parents had set up for me. I didn't have access to it until I turned 21, so she didn't see the point in telling me about it sooner. I then found myself a young college student with an abundance of money -- and almost no family. I would trade one for the other any day.

I used the money from the trust fund to pay off Aunt Marion's mortgage, which was the least I could do for the woman who raised me. I also paid off the student loans I had from getting my Bachelor's degree, and was able to pay for law school. And then, while visiting Tessa in New York, in her studio apartment that she shared with two other girls, I went shopping and didn't look at price tags. I couldn't believe how empowering it was to feel confident in how I looked. A passion for fashion was ignited in me that day. I stood proud on 4" heels and owned my height for the first time ever. I bought silk and cashmere and leather . . . I have accumulated quite the collection at this point.

When I moved into my townhouse three years ago, I took a small room off the master bedroom and turned it into a giant closet. It has hardwood floors with an animal print throw rug sprawling the open space. The walls and the shelves are all painted a soft white. The only pops of color are the handbags and shoes, which are displayed like the art that they are on the floor to ceiling shelves. There is an island with a white marble top centered in the room. The drawers, which are painted hot pink, are where I keep a lot of smaller clutches, scarves and jewelry. I hung a gold chandelier above the island, which sets the closet aglow, and makes the space warm and inviting. A chair with gold metallic arms and legs and a white furry seat and seatback sits in the corner. It's a great spot to sit and put on shoes. I could live in the closet. So could Tessa.

Tessa walks into the closet and sighs. "This is just pure heaven," she says. "I don't know what to look at first." She picks up a Chanel clutch, "I'll be bringing this little love with me tonight," she says while hugging the bag.

I just laugh at her. "What are you feeling tonight – dress? Jeans? What do you think?" I ask her.

"Dress. Definitely. And you know I'm limited to what will fit me. You and those long legs – it's not fair," Tessa says. "Dresses are over here?" She asks heading to a corner of the closet.

"Yeah, they're all over there. They are color coordinated. Grab whatever you want. That cobalt blue dress would look fabulous on you." I tell her.

After much back and forth and trying things on, we both decide on our outfits. I wear black skinny jeans and a black silk camisole with an open back. I wear my leopard print pumps and bring a hot pink clutch. Tessa after trying on 10 dresses decides to wear the very first one she tried on, the cobalt blue dress. The dress is short with long fitted sheer sleeves. Tessa pins the bottom of the dress up so that it's the length she likes – which is *very* short. She brought her own black peep toe booties and carries the gold Chanel bag. It's 9:30 when we're finally ready to go. I make a point to set the alarm and lock the door on the way out. I'm not taking any chances.

We head to Ice, a club in the Meatpacking District. Tessa, of course, knows someone that swoops us past the long line and in some type of back door. The music is pounding my ears and there are lights flashing everywhere – it's truly an assault on the senses. Tessa grabs my hand and leads me to the packed dance floor where we start dancing as the DJ spins some new techno/rock music. I let myself get lost in the beat of the music and the rhythm of the crowd. After a few long songs, Tessa grabs my hand and is trying to yell something to me.

"What?!" I shout back.

She gets right up to my ear and yells, "Let's go – we have a table." She points toward a roped off section.

Tessa somehow forces a path through the sea of people on the dance floor. As we near our table it thankfully quiets down and although my ears are still ringing a little, it is much more calm.

"I need a drink. It's crazy out there, right?!" Tessa says as she flags a server. "A bottle of Grey Goose, a bottle of tonic, a bowl of ice and a bowl of limes, please."

"We're turning to vodka now? You mean business tonight," I say with a smile.

"I'm sweating and thirsty and it will be refreshing. Besides, at these tables, it's bottle service only."

"Oh, right. This DJ is actually pretty good. That was fun!" I say, and really mean it. "I think I did need this night out – I haven't felt this good in weeks!"

"Wow the alcohol must be getting to you – you actually said something positive! It's a girl's night miracle!" Tessa says laughing as she hands me one of the two glasses she has been expertly preparing. "Cheers to us! And to that incredibly hot guy behind you." Although she is holding her glass up to cheers mine, she is looking right through me.

I instinctively start to turn around to see who she's ogling – but Tessa grabs my arm and whisper yells, "Don't turn around! I don't want him to know I'm talking about him!"

"Oh. Okay, relax! Jeez! Why don't you just go over there?"

Before Tessa can scold me anymore, a tall, dark, handsome guy is by our side. He can't stop smiling at Tessa.

"Hi there" says the stranger. "My name is Michal. Want to dance?" He asks in a foreign accent as he runs his hands through his dark hair.

And they're off. I sit back down at the table, sipping my vodka tonic as I watch the crowd gyrating to the beat.

After a few songs Tessa and Michal come rushing back to the table, out of breath and laughing. Tessa sits down on the couch side of the table with me, which faces out toward the dance floor, and Michal and a friend sit opposite us in big comfy leather chairs.

"V – this is Michal's friend Jarka. They're from the Czech Republic." Tessa says as she makes more vodka tonics.

"Hi there." I say, perhaps a little unenthusiastically. I offer a weak smile as Jarka sits down across from me and extend my hand for a handshake. Bypassing the handshake, Jarka stands up and comes over to my side of the table. He grabs my shoulders, leans in and plants a kiss on each cheek, as I sit stiffly. He then sits back down with a goofy smile on his face. I shake that off, and then reach over to shake Michal's hand. Since he's further away, he just grabs my hand and kisses the back of it.

Okay – so they're into kissing. I look at Tessa who is bubbling over with enthusiasm and she whispers in my ear, "Aren't they just the cutest?!"

I nod my head trying to feign excitement, but she sees right through me. "Just try and have fun, for me. Please?" She says.

"Of course!" I say. And I promise to give the two Czechs a chance.

We spend the next few hours hanging out with Michal and Jarka, and they actually seem like pretty good guys. Not my type, but they appear to be harmless. Michal is definitely into Tessa big time, and I'm pretty sure the feeling is mutual.

Michal asks Tessa to dance and they head out to the dance floor. Jarka and I are now sitting at the table in an awkward silence. "Verity, would you like to dance?" Jarka asks tentatively.

"Sure. Why not." I answer. And honestly, why not?

Although I hate to admit it, it's fun dancing with a partner out on the crazy dance floor. At least no random weirdos try and grind up on me. But after a few songs –the vodka I've been drinking at the table all night starts to catch up with me, and the room begins to spin. I need to sit down.

"I need to sit down," I yell to Jarka. He nods his head, takes my hand and leads me up to the table. I sit on the couch with a thump. "I need water."

Jarka flags a waiter down and asks for water. When the water comes I drink the glass in large gulps. The cool liquid feels so good on my parched throat. I look at my phone and it's 1 a.m. I want to go home. But how am I going to get Tessa's attention? I try waving to her, but she is not looking up toward the table.

"Jarka, do you think you could go get Tessa for me?" I ask.

"Of course. I'll be right back."

Once Jarka leaves, I close my eyes for a minute to try and stop the room from spinning. It doesn't really help. I open my eyes and I know I've had too much to drink when I see Ryker Rensselaer standing right in front of me.

"Verity. Are you okay?" He asks, looking legitimately concerned.

"Ryker?! What are you doing here?"

He sits down next to me on the couch. "This is one of my clubs. I try and stop by at least once a weekend. I definitely have never seen you here before," he says surprised.

"I'm surprised too," I say with a laugh. "A friend dragged me out."

"I saw your friends. Who are the Europeans with the long hair and skinny jeans?" Ryker asks, annoyed.

"They are from the Czech Republic," I say, finding this very amusing. "Their names are Michal and Jarka - and they are very sweet."

"Well now I know you've had too much to drink," Ryker jokes. "I can't imagine you trying to make small talk with those guys, never mind finding them sweet."

"Well, to be honest, my friend, Tessa, is really into Michal. I'm doing it for her. You know, like a 'wingman' type thing. Or is it 'wingwoman'?" I say, confused.

"Verity Townshend, the wingman?! Well, you really are making my night," Ryker says, unable to stop laughing. I start laughing too, and soon the two of us are hysterical.

Tessa comes running up to the table. She stops short when she sees Ryker and I sitting next to each other on the couch uncontrollably laughing. A huge smile spreads across her face, and she says "So Verity, are you going to introduce me to your new friend, or what?"

Catching my breath, I wipe the tears from my eyes. "Oh, he's not a new friend, I've known him for a while now. This is Ryker Rensselaer. We work together." And then I turn to Ryker, "Ryker, this is my best friend, Tessa."

Ryker stands up and offers Tessa his hand. She encloses his hand in both of hers, shaking it, not taking her eyes off him.

"Ryker, huh? I think I've heard V mention you. Big real estate guy, right?"

Tessa still hasn't let go of Ryker's hand, and I know she wishes she could make direct eye contact with him, but even in 4" heels she barely reaches his shoulder.

"I'm so glad to hear that 'V' can't stop talking about me. Although I have to admit, she offers me so very little about her personal life, I didn't know if she had any friends, never mind a beautiful best friend named Tessa."

With that line, Tessa gives Ryker his hand back. "Well, then you probably know her better than almost anyone else. She's a tough nut to crack. But once you do, it's totally worth it," Tessa says with a wink.

"Okay. That'll be enough chatting you two. Actually, Tessa, before I ran into Ryker, I was getting ready to leave."

Tessa glances behind her and I see Michal and Jarka pretending not to watch us from a distance.

"Just give me one minute," she says, "and then I'll get the server to send us the bill."

"This one is on the house, in celebration of me meeting Verity's best friend," Ryker says, looking over at me.

"Ryker, that is not necessary. Really." I start to proteset.

"If the man wants to pay – let the man pay, Verity! It's nice to know there are still gentlemen in this city," Tessa says. "Thank you very much, Ryker. And it was an absolute pleasure meeting you."

Tessa bounces away to see Michal and a dejected looking Jarka.

I turn to Ryker, "It's not easy for me to accept things like this from people, so thank you. You definitely made Tessa's night – she thought she was going to have to pay for this VIP table," I say, and we both start laughing.

"It's nothing, really. You should come here more often – if you do, maybe I'll even let you pay."

"But probably not," I say, which gets another chuckle out of Ryker.

Tessa is back with Michal's number entered into her phone.

"Follow me," Ryker says. I stay close behind Ryker and hold Tessa's hand as Ryker leads us through a private area in the back of the club, and around to the back entrance we came in.

"From now on, when you come here, you come in this entrance and say my name" Ryker says.

"We came in this way tonight," I say, a little matter-of-factly.

"Well, aren't you just full of surprises, 'V'" Ryker says amused.

And I don't know if it's the alcohol, the music, the lights, or a combination of the three, but I spontaneously reach up on my tiptoes and plant a kiss on Ryker's cheek, pausing for a minute so I can smell his musky aftershave. He stands there with a stunned look on his face, unable to move. Then Tessa and I giggle as we go out the door and into the cool September night.

Chapter 9

The sun is streaming through the window and directly into my eyes. I definitely was too out of it to remember to close the drapes last night. Rolling over, I hide my head under a mountain of pillows, trying to fall back asleep, but my body won't let me. The positive side to drinking too much – blackout sleep! No nightmares. Although, feeling like I do right now, it's not worth it.

My head hurts. I lift up the covers and see that, yes, I'm still in my black jeans and black silk top. Wow - I haven't had a night like that in a *long* time. Aspirin and water, right now. Peeling the covers off, I swing my legs around and try the sitting position for a minute. With much effort, I slowly push myself to standing, and then notice there are 2 aspirin and a glass from my kitchen filled with water. Tessa, maybe? I'm pretty positive I wasn't capable of such forethought last night.

Gulping down the aspirin and some water, I pause for a minute to let my head catch up with my body. Somehow I make it down the hall, and see the guest room door is wide open. Glancing into the room, Tessa is laying on top of the covers, still in the cobalt blue dress. Yikes. At least she got her shoes off.

"Knock, knock," I say as I lightly knock on the open door. "Tessa, are you awake?" I ask, knowing full well she's not even close to awake.

"Yeah, I'm awake. I'm awake. What time is it?" Tessa says, her voice thick with sleep.

"I think it's about 8:30."

"8:30? Why the heck are you awake so early? And more importantly, why are you waking me up so early?!" Tessa is not a morning person - at all.

"Sorry! I forgot to shut my drapes last night so the sun was shining right in my face. Can you believe we both fell asleep in our clothes?" I say with a laugh.

Tessa sits up and starts laughing. I walk over and sit on the end of the bed. "How did we even get home last night? Did we take a cab?" I ask her.

"Wow, you really don't remember anything, do you?! Ryker had his driver bring us home. You remember Ryker, right? And what you did right as we were leaving?" Tessa asks me with a gleam in her eye.

"Oh god. I kissed him. This is bad. How am I going to work with him now?! I should not be allowed to drink vodka. I'm a wine drinker – what was I thinking?!"

"Oh stop! You had fun for once in your life! Don't ruin it. Last night was epic," Tessa says grinning. "Why was Ryker there anyway? Coincidence?"

"He owns the club," I tell her, and for some strange reason I'm a little embarrassed.

"Whoa! What?! That's amazing! We are going every weekend," Tessa says.

"Speaking of amazing - what about Michal?! He seemed really into you."

"He was adorable, right?! And by leaving when I did, I totally left him wanting more," Tessa says matter-of-factly. Over the years, I have heard Tessa repeatedly rattle off a variety of different rules and theories about men and dating. And although I tend to laugh at her, and even roll my eyes sometimes, she must be on to something, because she always has a slew of men after her.

"Let's change into comfy clothes and go downstairs for coffee. I don't think I've ever needed coffee so bad in my life," I say. "Oh, and thanks so much for getting me that aspirin and water last night - that was so thoughtful! Now if you had only just shut my drapes we would both be sleeping soundly right now," I tease.

"Um, I'd love to take credit for the aspirin and water, but that wasn't me. You saw me this morning – I barely got my shoes off."

"Huh. That's odd. Maybe I did it? But, I was in the same shape as you," I say pointing at my outfit. "Weird."

After changing into cashmere sweats and a soft long sleeve t-shirt, I slip into my fuzzy slippers and head downstairs to start the coffee. Tessa comes down a few minutes later in some of my clothes. Even as the sun shines through the window, and the kitchen is filled with the heavenly smell of coffee, Tessa and I look at each other, feeling miserable. The two clutches we brought out last night are strewn on the counter -credit cards, cash, cell phones and lip gloss are spilling out everywhere. We look at the mess and then back at each other, and we burst into a fit of laughter. We're laughing so hard tears are streaming down our cheeks and my sides ache. Sometimes the morning after is even more memorable than the night of.

"Okay, so here's the plan," Tessa says once we calm down. "We have a cup of coffee here, and then we are going down the street to Sarabeth's for brunch. We'll stuff our faces with greasy food and bloody mary's."

"You are crazy. But I don't want to cook – so Sarabeth's it is."

"I'm crazy? You're crazy. Do you know when we got home last night your front door wasn't even locked?! Who lives in a multi-million dollar townhouse alone and doesn't lock their front door?"

"Wait. What? I know for a fact that I locked the door when we left last night. I set the alarm and locked the door. I'm sure of it. Oh no," I groan. "This isn't the first time this has happened."

"Really? Maybe the lock is broken. You should get a locksmith to come take a look at it," Tessa says as she pours what seems like a gallon of milk and ten sugars into the mug with her coffee.

I shake my head, "I know it's not the lock. Strange things have been happening lately. Things I can't explain."

"What do you mean? What kind of things?"

"I don't really want to get into it right now. I'm probably just overthinking it," I say dismissively.

"You, overthink something? I don't believe it," Tessa says, her voice dripping with sarcasm.

Tessa and I spend the day going out for brunch, which includes a bloody mary for her and a mimosa for me. And although I thought she was nuts wanting more alcohol, I actually think it made me feel better. Not that I'll ever tell her that.

After brunch, we attempt to go into a few boutiques near the restaurant, but our hearts aren't in it. Neither of us feels like trying clothes on right now. So we go back to my house, collapse on my couch and watch movies all afternoon. It's a nice change for me, but I also feel a little guilty for being so unproductive. I can't help but always feel like I need to spend every minute of every day doing . . . something. I know this feeling is driven by the fear that life can end at any moment. I just don't want to waste any time. I say as much to Tessa as she scrolls through the movie list on Netflix looking for a romantic comedy, and she rolls her eyes at me and tells me I need to "seriously relax." I'm sure she's right; she usually is.

Chapter 10

My heart hammers in my chest as I race through a hallway that never ends. With each turn around a corner, the hallway in front of me only gets longer, and my breathing gets more labored. I can hear him behind me, grunting and angry. My legs are like lead and won't move as fast as they need to. I turn the next corner as quickly as my numb body will go, and I almost smack dead into a wall. I turn around and around looking for another escape route- - but now all four walls are closing in on me. There's no way out and he's coming. I can feel the heat from his body and can smell a sickeningly sweet smell. I try to scream but my lungs are now filled with water and I begin to choke. He's here. Now too scared to scream - I just want to cry.

I jolt awake and throw my hands up to my throat, coughing as if water fills my lungs. Making a conscious effort to slow down my breathing, I take in deep breaths while resting against my headboard. Cracking my eyes open to slits, I see the world is still dark - it must be before dawn. The clock on my nightstand reads 5:41, wow that's early.

Determined to turn this morning around, I get dressed in a pair of spandex yoga pants in a deep purple color and a gray long sleeve running top. Down in the gym in the lower level of my house, I turn on a morning news show, and do a half hour of cardio on my elliptical machine. After that nightmare, running does not appeal to me this morning. I then do some exercises with my free weights and finish with some ab work. It feels good to push against the weights and feel strong and capable. By the end of the hour- long workout, I feel like myself again.

With my coffee from Roast in hand, I skip the office and head straight to Greenwich Village - to Jane Street. I'm meeting Josh and his brother, Johnny, at the building to do a walk through and discuss the plans. On the cab ride downtown I decide to give David a call and see how things are going with the permit process. I'm pretty sure he was avoiding me at his office on Friday. David is usually in the office early, but his office line rings and rings until his voicemail picks up. I leave a brief message asking him to call me back. I then call his cell phone, and that goes to voicemail as well. I leave a similar message and can't help but start to worry about this permit issue. This could set our plans back for weeks, maybe even longer. My dream to have children enjoying the holidays at the CFF Home hangs in the balance.

Down at Jane Street, Josh is already walking around the space when I arrive.

"I see you got the key I sent," I say to Josh.

Josh jumps a little at the abrupt sound of my voice.

"Ah, yes. You startled me," he says with a slight chuckle at himself.

"This place will do that to you. There's definitely a spooky vibe in here, don't you think?"

"Not that I can feel," Josh says. "But I don't believe in spooky stuff. If I can't see it, it doesn't exist. I was just so focused on the plans for this amazing space. I have so many ideas. I can't wait to get started."

"Well let me hear your thoughts," I say, curious.

Thinking about what happened in the kitchen on Saturday, I say, "let's start in what will be the entryway. I'd love to hear what you can add to the architect's plans to functionally use the space as a lobby, but make it still feel like the entrance to a home."

"Absolutely. Follow me."

As we approach the entryway, a young man with dark hair neatly trimmed and big green eyes steps through the door.

"Hi there," he says, flashing a killer smile.

"Well, hello," I say, unable to keep from smiling back at him.

"Oh, right. Verity Townsend, this is Johnny, my younger, less handsome brother."

Johnny reaches his hand out and I grab it in a firm handshake. I know his type already, and I want to be clear from the beginning that I am all business.

"It's nice to meet you, Johnny. I have seen your carpentry work at the Tribeca apartment, and I have to say, I'm impressed. You are very talented."

"Thank you very much. And that's only the tip of the iceberg; my talents go deeper than you can imagine. Maybe I could show you some time?" Johnny says with too much of a gleam in his eyes.

"Never going to happen," I say matter-of-factly. I then turn my back to Johnny and give my attention to Josh who is shaking his head. "Josh, shall we continue?"

"Yes, of course, Verity. Please excuse my brother, I think he has inhaled too much dust on the job site."

Josh and I continue to discuss our ideas as we walk all three levels of the townhouse. I have avoided the kitchen successfully up to this point, but we have covered every inch of the rest of the building, so there's not much more stalling I can do.

"I think all that's left to see is the kitchen, right? Are you still okay to continue or are you running out of steam?" Josh asks.

I see that he is giving me an out, that 90% of me wants to take, but the professional in me won't allow it.

"Of course, I'm fine. Let's finish up!" I say with forced enthusiasm.

Just then my cell phone rings. I look and see that it's David Cohen, returning my call.

Excusing myself, I walk toward the front door to speak privately.

"David! It's great to hear from you. Thank you for getting back to me. I have to admit, I felt as though you may have been avoiding me all week." As Josh says, I don't beat around the bush.

"Hello, Verity. Yes, I was waiting to call you back until I had some answers. However, I think you'll forgive me once you hear this. I have great news. My expediter friend has self-certified the building plans and we are free to move forward!"

"Oh my gosh, David. That is excellent news! Thank you so much. This is truly such a relief!"

"I apologize for holding you in suspense for so long. I hope I didn't cause you and Evelyn too much stress," David says sincerely.

"Well you totally made up for it," I tell him, "Now, what is the next step?"

"Now the contractor has to go apply for a permit. He can do it himself, or he might have his own expediter that handles that for him. And then we are ready to begin construction."

"Okay, great. I'm with the contractor now. I will see if he can get this done today, and maybe we can start work tomorrow. Thank you again, David!"

After I hang up with David I go looking for Josh. Assuming he's in the kitchen, I head down the hall, but the sound of two male voices stops me short of walking in. The two men, who must be Josh and Johnny, talk in brusque tones to each other.

"I said I would handle it," Johnny says angrily, while trying to keep his voice down.

"Well, then handle it. You know the deal – make your decision," Josh says firmly back to him.

"Hi guys," I say, announcing my arrival. I walk into the kitchen slowly, "is everything okay?"

"Verity. Yes, it's fine. It's just business. You know what they say about working with family, right?" Josh says trying to laugh it off.

But Johnny is having a harder time pretending to be okay. He gives me a weak half smile, and places the glass of water he's drinking on the counter. "Verity, it was a pleasure meeting you and I look forward to working with you on this special project. But you'll have to excuse me, I've got some business to attend to."

"That looked pretty heated. Are we going to have a problem with the two of you working together?" I ask Josh.

"No, this is old news that should have been dealt with a long time ago. It should be over with today. I'm sorry you had to see that. But, how about your phone call? Is everything okay with you?" Josh says clearly trying to change the subject.

"Ah, yes. It's better than okay. We just got the city's approval on the building plans and we can start the work!"

"Wow! That is great news! Huge news for everyone, actually!" Josh says.

"I know, it is quite a relief. Now, all that needs to happen is for you to go apply for your permit. Once that permit is approved, we can get your crew in here right away. So, do you think you could go apply for the permit today? I think you mentioned some sort of miracle expediter you use?" I ask hopefully.

"I really appreciate your straightforward approach to everything, Verity. Yes, since we pretty much went over the whole house this morning, I can definitely go see my expediter, and hopefully we can start work tomorrow or Wednesday."

"Tomorrow would be better, of course."

"This project is my number one priority. I'm on it."

"Alright then. Just keep me updated as things unfold with your expediter, and have your crew ready to go!" I call after him as he leaves.

Just then I hear a loud crash. I spin around and see the glass of water Johnny was drinking is smashed on the kitchen floor. Shattered glass sparkles on the tile. The temperature drops and my hair stands on end. Another bang makes me whip around in the other direction toward the door, which has slammed shut. But the room is still. Deadly still. There is no wind to blame this time. She's here. The walls seem to be closing in on me, like my most recent nightmare. I want to turn and run, but it's as if my legs are filled with sand.

"What?!" I weakly yell to the empty room. "What do you want from me?" My voice, stronger now, echoes in the hollow house.

Chapter 11

I thank Frank and head out of Roast, almost bounding with excitement. Josh's expediter came through yesterday and work should start on Jane Street today! I can hardly contain myself. Now that we are on schedule, my plan to have the majority of the work done by Christmas should be possible. I am going to throw the most fabulous holiday party/fundraiser at the CFF Home – New York City won't know what hit it.

It's a warm morning for mid-September and that only adds to my good mood. I am dressed in what I consider 'smart casual' - a pair of dark skinny jeans, fitted down to the ankle, an oversized gray cashmere sweater, a blush pink scarf, and suede taupe ankle boots. I am ready for a day of work on site. Once I arrive at Jane Street, I am thrilled to see construction trucks lining the street.

Walking through the unlocked door, I hear the bustle of men talking, hammering, and banging. The sounds are a stark difference to the echoing emptiness that filled these walls yesterday. Josh has gone through and spray-painted a large 'X' on any wall that should come down, and three men are already taking an ax to one of those walls.

With a deep breath, I timidly open the kitchen door. Josh is across the room showing a short, thick man some plans on his iPad. He sees me across the room and smiles.

"Verity, you're here. Is this exciting, or what?"

"Josh, I am so pleased to see that you and your men have already gotten started. And don't worry, I'm not here to get in your way, but I will be working for a little while on my laptop. I will probably do this for a few days, in case there are any problems that I can help solve quickly. And to be honest, I just really want to be a part of it!"

"No problem at all! You of course can stay as long as you like, for as many days as you like. I will let you know if any questions come up."

Since the crew is focusing on demolishing the first level today, I bring my bag with my laptop upstairs. One of the bedrooms has an old desk chair that I wheel over close to the window so I have some natural light, and a little bit of a view of Jane Street. Propping my laptop on my lap, I plug in my mobile hotspot and start by checking my emails. I then send out an email to the members of the Board of Directors with the exciting update. Almost immediately, I get responses back from Mitchell, Ryker, Chip and David – all with congratulatory remarks and full of positive feedback.

About an hour into my work Josh peeks his head into the room. "Verity, there you are."

"Oh, hi Josh. Is everything okay?"

"Yes, absolutely. I just wanted to let you know, I'm going to run out to get a few supplies really quick. Can I get you anything?"

"No, I'm fine. I probably will head up to the CFF office soon, but thank you."

"Of course," Josh says, "I told the guys to come to you with any questions, since you know the plans as well, if not better, than me at this point."

About 45 minutes later, there's a light knock on the open door to the bedroom. "Excuse me, Ms. Townsend?"

I turn around and see the short, stout man Josh had been talking to downstairs at the door.

"Yes, hello. Please, call me Verity. What can I help you with . . . What was your name?"

"Yes, Ms. Verity. I am Gino," he says in a thick Brooklyn accent. "I have a question about something on the plans, would you mind coming downstairs to the kitchen with me? I just want to make double sure we're doing the right thing."

Once we reach the kitchen, Gino says, "Okay, I actually have two questions. The kitchen door, it doesn't have an "X" on it, but I think in the plans you wanted it taken out. Is that correct?"

"Yes, you are correct. We want to create a more open feel."

"Okay, that's what I thought. Also, do you see this wall over here?" Gino walks over to the wall next to the kitchen door. "It's not on the plans, but if you really want to open up the doorway area, I was thinking we could cut into this wall and double the size of the doorway. I can tell it's not original to the house anyway. It's drywall, not plaster. We could frame out a new, wider doorway. It would be a really nice entrance into the back of the house."

"I think that's a great idea. I don't know why I didn't think of it. Let's do it," I say with a smile.

"Great." Gino says, obviously proud of himself. "Should I wait to run this by Mr. Mesa or can we go ahead while we're already doing some demo back here?"

"No need to wait, go right ahead and start on it. If Mr. Mesa has any questions, you can tell him to ask me about it."

Gino turns around and shouts, "Mikey, come over here. Take this door out and part of this wall. I'll mark it for you."

I realize there is about to be a lot of noise, so I decide to escape back upstairs. I then hear some loud banging as they continue the demo.

After a few minutes, I become so focused on my work, I am immune to the constant banging and sawing going on downstairs. I tune it out like white noise. But then, the noise stops dead. Everything is quiet - too quiet. A man yelling in a panicked voice interrupts the unnatural silence.

My body tenses as I sense the ... terror. Something is horribly wrong. With no time to think, I jump up from my chair, knocking my laptop to the floor with a crash that reverberates through the stillness. I race downstairs and down the hallway toward the kitchen, my breath coming out in short, panicked spurts. I see that the door into the kitchen has been knocked down as planned. Through the now open doorway, I see five of the construction workers facing me, shocked into silence. They are all staring toward the wall next to the doorway; stock still, with eyes wide with horror at what is in front of them.

I stop running as I get closer to the door. I slowly walk through the demolition debris, half knowing, and half afraid. I turn my head to follow the stares of the men, with flashes from my nightmares filling my brain - the fearful round eyes, the blue lips and bloated hands.

And then I see her. Her limp body is contorted half in, half out of the wall. Her straggly hair is full of dust and plaster. One arm is awkwardly pinned under her body and the other is strewn over her head. She is bent at the waist, with her legs and feet still inside the bottom half of the wall which hasn't been removed yet.

My throat closes and I can't catch my breath. The room gets cold and I smell that sick sweet smell. As the world starts to go black I simultaneously hear Gino, "Ms. Verity, are you okay?" and Josh's voice "Hey, what's going on in here? Why has all the work stopped?"

And I'm out.

Chapter 12

"I think she's coming to – her eyes just flickered."

"Someone go get her some water."

I slowly open my eyes, letting in little bits of light at a time. I can't remember what happened yet, but I know I'm not ready for reality. I see Josh, Gino, more construction workers, and men in suits hovering around the room. The mood is grim and serious, and I now remember why. The girl.

I sit up and I'm immediately nauseous. I close my eyes again and take a deep breath.

"Verity, here, drink some water." Josh is staring at me, and I can tell he has no idea what to do with an emotional woman. I take a small sip from the glass. I don't think I'm going to throw up, so that's a relief.

"Verity, are you okay? You scared me to death," Josh says. With the mention of the word 'death' we stop and stare at each other, silently communicating the unspeakable.

"I'm okay. Who are all these people?" I ask looking around at the packed room.

"It's the police, Verity. NYPD Detectives, crime scene people, the coroner . . ."

"Oh my god. This is real."

Josh nods his head.

A tall man, about 6'4", with broad shoulders and a full head of graying dark hair approaches us. He's got large, brown eyes, and a round face with permanent dimples, which were probably adorable at one time.

"Hello, Ms. Townsend. I'm Detective Brendan O'Donnell, NYPD. Can I ask you a few questions?"

"Maybe we could give her a few minutes," Josh says.

"No, it's okay. Really. I'd rather get this over with."

"Thank you, Ms. Townsend. Why don't you come sit on this chair over here," Detective O'Donnell says.

The two men help me stand up, and my legs almost fail me again. I grab on to both Josh and the Detective's arms and somehow make my way over to the chair. It's the chair from the bedroom upstairs; someone must have brought it down. I am grateful for the seat, and am trying to focus, but too many thoughts are swirling through my brain.

"Who is she? Does anyone know who she is?" I ask abruptly. It's important to me that I know her name.

"We'll get to that," O'Donnell says, and then turning to Josh says, "Mr. Mesa, would you excuse us please." But it's not a question.

"Okay Ms. Townsend, why don't we start with you telling me what happened. Everything you can remember before you passed out."

I take a deep breath. "Um, okay. I was upstairs in the first bedroom sitting in this chair, actually, and working on my laptop. Then all the loud noise from the construction work completely stops. The sudden silence had me worried so I stood up, and then I think I heard a man yell. I'm not sure what he said, but the tone of his voice made me run down the stairs. And then I came into the kitchen, and I saw her. Her hair, and her arm. . ."

A shiver crawls up my spine and I shake my head in an attempt to shake out the image of her body. "Then I think I passed out," I tell him. "That's really all that I can remember. I'm sorry I can't be more helpful."

"No, you're doing great. Who do you remember seeing before you passed out?" the Detective asks.

"I saw Gino, and a few more of the construction workers. And I think Josh, too."

"Thank you, Ms. Townsend. I may need to come back to you at some point. In the meantime, if you think of anything – no matter how small the detail, please give me a call," Detective O'Donnell says as he hands me his business card.

"Ok. Of course," I tell him. "But please, would you mind telling me her name? It's important to me."

"We aren't quite sure of the young woman's identity yet. I will let you know when the information is available," Detective O'Donnell says in a somber voice. And then he walks over to speak to a man in a navy jacket with the word "Coroner" written in bright yellow letters across the back.

Searching for air, and the courage to call Evelyn, I find myself outside on Jane Street. While pacing up and down the sidewalk, I glance up at the cloudless blue sky, which reminds me of my excitement from this morning. Only a few hours ago I rushed down to Jane Street on this beautiful day, filled with hope and joy. That now seems like a lifetime ago. Hearing the chatter and laughter from passers-by, I'm envious of their blissful ignorance.

It's not going to get any easier, I think with a sigh, and pull out my phone to call Evelyn.

"Hello! Verity! How are things over on Jane Street?" Evelyn answers in a cheery voice.

"Evelyn, there's something I need to tell you."

Chapter 13

Curling up on my couch in my comfiest sweats, I wrap myself in a soft blanket, and watch the flames dance in the hearth. Growing up I always had a real wood fireplace, which I prefer, but I found it to be impractical in the city. And I have to admit - I really enjoy having an instant fire with the flip of a switch. Even with my sweatpants, blanket, blazing fire and mug of steamy peppermint tea, I still can't seem to shake the chill that has settled in my bones. The only noise comes from the crackling flames, which have put me in a trance as flashes of the girl's body burn my brain.

Evelyn responded better than expected to the news of a dead body being found in the walls of CFF's new home for children. Of course, she was shocked, horrified, even speechless at one point, but she didn't faint – so that's better than I handled it. Evelyn expressed concern for me, since of course this is not the first dead body I've seen, and she offered to come visit me at home. When I told her I really just needed to be alone – to go home and rest, she understood. I've been sitting here in front of the fire ever since.

Evelyn offered to inform the Board members, an offer I gratefully accepted. The thought of repeating this story over and over again – I think I would have completely lost it.

I can't help but wonder about this woman. Who exactly is she? How long ago was she murdered? *How* was she murdered? And then, although I feel a little guilty about it, I'm also concerned about the more practical things, like how will this affect the charity? How long of a setback will our construction timetable suffer? And how will the negative press effect donations and support for CFF? Could the past few years of work all be for naught? Is the whole project ruined? I am overwhelmed by distress and despair, but tears will not come. I'm afraid if and when I ever do start to cry, I won't be able to stop. For now, I'm thankful for the shock-induced numbness.

I'm running down a shadowy alley, my breathing is labored but I must keep going. It's dark and cold. With each exhale, my breath puffs out in a steamy mist. My shoes silently pound the dirt beneath my feet faster and faster. All I hear is his heavy grunting, which sounds angry, and scared – and gaining on me. My heavy skirts begin to drag on the ground, so I reach down to hold them up, and I'm thrown off balance. I trip and fall and almost immediately he's on top of me. I scramble and manage to flip around, now crawling backwards as fast as my body will go. My back bumps into something hard and brick, stopping me short. He lifts me up and swiftly throws me over the brick edge. The world starts flying by, as the light above me grows smaller. I'm f a l l i n g . . .and then I hit the water, and the world goes black.

I wake with a jump. My heart is racing and my stomach is in my throat as if I've just been on a rollercoaster and I'm speeding down a steep decline. I sit up and look around, trying to get my bearings. I'm home. I'm okay. The fire is still blazing and I'm sweating under my blanket. I rip it off and feel the heat escape my body. I have never had a falling nightmare like that one. However, considering today's events, I'm not surprised I had a nightmare. I look at the clock and it's almost 7:30 p.m. –

my whole house is dark, the only light coming from the fire. Just then, my doorbell rings.

I trudge over to my front door, still a bit disoriented. I turn on the kitchen lights on my way, and peer through the peephole. There is a large man on my front stoop in a black overcoat with his back to the door. My heart starts to race again - I'm just going to pretend I'm not home.

The man turns back around to ring the bell again and I see that it's Detective O'Donnell. Why would he be here at this time of night? I unlock the door and open it just enough to let my face show.

"Detective O'Donnell? What are you doing here?" I ask.

"Ms. Townsend, you're here." He says with a look of relief on his face. "I apologize for the late hour, but I would really like to speak with you. Could I come in for a few minutes?"

Although I'm not at all in the mood to talk, I let out a big sigh and open the door all the way.

"Please, come on in," I say and lead him to the kitchen. "Have a seat at the counter if you'd like. Can I offer you something to drink? I was about to make myself some tea."

"No, thank you," the Detective answers politely. "Again, I apologize for just showing up on your doorstep, but I tried calling you a few times, and when you didn't answer, I got worried."

"I'm sorry, I turned my phone off. I haven't been in the mood to talk to anyone. But worried? Why would you be worried about me?" I ask.

"Ms. Townsend" Detective O'Donnell starts.

"Please, call me Verity," I interrupt him.

"Verity, I was worried about you."

Mid-pour, I stop filling my teakettle with water and stare at Detective O'Donnell trying to wrap my head around what he's saying.

"Why would you be worried about me? Shouldn't you be focused on finding a murderer?"

"You find the body of a young dead woman, and then hours go by and I can't get ahold of you. It's my job to worry about things like that," he says.

"Can you tell me who she was?"

"Her name was Chloe Kingston. We matched her description to a missing persons report that was filed two days ago, and DNA has confirmed it."

I take minute to let the now identified woman's name sink in: Chloe Kingston.

"Are there any suspects?"

"It's still very early in the investigation – we have a lot that we're looking at. "Did you know Josh Mesa knew Ms. Kingston?"

Trying to hide my surprise, I just repeatedly dip my tea bag into the steaming water. Words can't seem to find their way to my brain or out of my mouth.

"How did he know her?" I manage to squeak out.

"She did some work for him. She was an interior designer."

"Well, I don't know Josh very well, but he does not appear to be the murdering type," I tell him with a shaky voice. "And we just closed on the Jane Street property this past Friday. It's only been a few days since CFF has owned the building," I say, defending the charity. "Maybe you should be looking into the former owner of the building. I mean, do you even know how long her body had been in the wall?"

The Detective just nods his head. "We're working on that. When was the first time you entered the building after the charity purchased it?"

"Let's see, I went there Saturday morning to do a walk-through with Evelyn and Ryker."

Detective O'Donnell flips open a notepad. "Now, that would be Evelyn Campbell and Ryker Rensselaer?"

"Yes." My heart skips a beat at the mention of Ryker's name.

"Okay," the Detective responds, as he writes something down in his notebook. "Was that the only time you were in the building until this morning?"

"No. I was also there yesterday to meet with Mr. Mesa to discuss the renovation plans."

"Was it just the two of you there yesterday morning?"

"Yes. Um, no. His brother Johnny showed up too. They work together. Josh is a contractor and Johnny is a carpenter," I explain.

Detective O'Donnell keeps writing, and I can tell he's going over the timeline.

"How many keys are there to the building?" he asks.

"There are five keys."

"Who has the five keys?"

"I just had keys made on Friday after the closing. I had four copies made, one for me, Evelyn, David Cohen, Ryker, and Josh Mesa."

"Ok, so you had one key, and then made four more," Detective O'Donnell confirms.

"Yes, that's right," I say looking into his serious brown eyes. The questions about the keys are starting to make me nervous. Is one of these people that I gave a key to a murderer? I go through the list in my head and decide - absolutely not.

"With all due respect, Detective, I know it's your job to look into everyone who had access to the building, but I know these people. I just don't see how any of them could be responsible for such a thing as murdering a young woman. It's just not possible," I say with conviction.

"I need to look into everyone and everything, if nothing more than to rule them out. You understand."

I nod my head.

"Would you happen to have a receipt from the locksmith that shows how many keys were made?"

"Yes, of course, at the office. Why, you don't believe me?" I say, clearly irritated.

"It's just procedure" he says calmly.

I want to tell him what he can do with his procedure, but he just keeps asking more questions.

"Who is David Cohen?" he asks.

"He is an attorney and a member of CFF's Board of Directors. He handled the closing of the purchase of Jane Street." I slowly sip my tea. I'm doing my best to get through this. "Are we almost done here?" I ask a little flippantly.

"Yes, we're almost done. Just a few more questions. When did you send David, Ryker and Josh their keys?"

"I messengered the keys to each of them Friday afternoon - maybe around 3 p.m."

Detective O'Donnell scribbles something into his notebook.

"How long have you known Mr. Mesa?" he asks.

"I only just met him last week. Ryker had a contractor for the job that fell through and he was referred to Mr. Mesa. Since time was a concern, I immediately went to meet with him and see one of his finished projects. I guess that was last Wednesday?"

"You seem to have really moved things along quickly with the purchase of the building and then an immediate start on the construction. That is no easy feat in this city. How exactly did you make this miracle happen?" As he asks, Detective O'Donnell sounds very casual and innocent, but I see right through that.

I slowly put my mug of tea down on the counter, and glare at the Detective across the island. "If you are insinuating that CFF used any illegal means to begin construction so quickly after the purchase, you can just leave right now." I can barely contain my anger.

"I'm not saying that at all. It's an innocent question, Verity. But I would like an answer."

"There's no miracle involved, just hard work, good planning, and maybe a bit of luck. It actually almost didn't even happen. David has an expediter friend who offered to do us a favor a while back. They said they would self-certify our work permit. But then David said there was some problem and the person might not be able to do it. You see, I would have liked to start work on Friday, right after the closing. But, as I said, there was some problem on David's end with his friend. And then, last minute on Monday the expediter came through. I then sent Mr. Mesa to acquire his permit so that we could begin work today." As I say it, I realize how long ago this morning seems. It was a whole lifetime ago.

Detective O'Donnell stands up and puts his notebook and pen into the inside pocket of his coat. He offers a small smile that shows his dimples and holds out his giant hand for me to shake, "Thank you, Verity. You have been very helpful. I can tell you want justice for Chloe Kingston just as much as I do."

I shake his hand. "Can I ask you something?"

"Yes," he answers.

"How did she die?"

"We're not exactly sure yet, and I wouldn't want to speculate without the facts. We'll need a little more time."

I nod my head.

"If you think of anything else, please contact me."

Following him to the front door, I see the Detective out and lock the door after he leaves. I double-check to make sure the alarm is set, and I head back to the kitchen.

I grab my steaming mug of tea and go sit back down by the fire. I stare into the dancing flames, with the heat emanating from the hearth and warming my skin. I keep going over and over the questions Detective O'Donnell asked me. It is all too real now. Someone I know is a murderer. But, why? Who would want to murder a young interior designer?

I have also realized that it has most likely been Chloe who I can feel around me at Jane Street, in elevators, and in my dreams (nightmares). She is asking me for help, even though I didn't know her. I'm not sure why she would come to me.

These thoughts weigh on me and I'm suddenly exhausted again. As I'm coming out of my brain fog, I hear my tummy rumble – I don't think I've had anything to eat since breakfast. I need to put some food in my body and then go to bed.

Back in the kitchen, I pour myself a bowl of cereal - the only meal I have energy to make right now. Adding a little almond milk to the bowl, I sit at the kitchen island taking bite after bite, like a robot, not even tasting the food. When I'm finished I put my bowl and spoon into the dishwasher, switch off the fire and the lights, and head up to bed - glad one of the worst days of my life is finally over.

Chapter 14

My eyes creep open to a pitch-black room. Leaving my warm nest of blankets is the last thing I want to do, but I know there's no way I'll fall back asleep. Once I'm up, I'm up. I should just get out of bed and get a workout in. Rolling over onto my back, I let out a whiny groan. It's definitely before 6 a.m. Checking my phone, it's confirmed, 5:20 a.m. Ugh.

Sluggishly, I pull my blankets off and sit for a minute. Yesterday's events come rushing back to me, and I now feel the need to sweat and clear my head. The nightmare where I'm chased still lingers in the back of my brain and it's dark and cold outside – so I decide to workout at home today. Blindly grabbing a pair of capri-length workout pants and a tank top out of my drawer, I quickly get changed. I think I need yoga.

Programming my favorite at-home yoga class onto my big screen television down in the gym, I lay down my mat and immediately begin to relax. Yoga had never been an interest of mine until recently. I had always preferred real heart-pounding cardio and weight workouts – like running, kick boxing, spinning – fast-paced programs. Then one of the CFF volunteers told me yoga was "life changing" and I just had to try it. Despite feeling like my life really didn't need changing, I decided I'd give it a shot. And now I understand. It really is a great addition to my exercise routine. There is something spiritual about yoga that I don't get from my other workouts.

After about an hour of stretching and breathing I feel dramatically better than I did when I woke up. I realize I need to call an emergency Board meeting for CFF, and I really need to talk to Evelyn about everything. And by that, I mean everything – nightmares and all.

For some reason Chloe has reached out to me for help, and I feel a connection to her that is unexplainable. I have to do whatever I can to find out who killed her and why. Although, I have no idea how I'm going to do that. One never knows what life is going to throw at you . . . or what is hiding in your walls.

After a quick shower and egg white and veggie omelet, I make my way over to Roast. While waiting for my coffee order, I send Evelyn a text about the need to call an emergency Board meeting today. As I'm stepping out of the cab in front of the CFF office building, I see Evelyn getting out of a cab right in front of mine. She couldn't sleep either.

"Evelyn" I call to her. She sees me and we meet in front of the building.

"Good morning."

"Well, I certainly wouldn't call it a good morning. How are you, Verity? What a traumatic experience you had yesterday. I am so sorry," Evelyn says, as she sympathetically looks into my eyes, searching for the answer to my true feelings.

I hand her the coffee I bought her, and give her a small smile. "I'm fine. We'll get through this," I tell her confidently. But right now, looking back into Evelyn's tired eyes, I'm not so sure. It's going to be a long day.

Up in the CFF office, Evelyn and I sit in the cheery sitting room drinking our coffees. I feel we both need to be surrounded by the sweet artwork created by the children of CFF – smiley-faced stick figures and colorful thank-you letters. All are a positive reminder of why we started the CFF Home project and why we need to fix all of this as soon as possible.

"Okay," I say to Evelyn. "Let's take emotion out of this for a minute. Let's think about this problem logically and methodically. First things first, we are going to have quite a public relations issue once this hits the media, which it probably has already. I didn't have time to look at the newspaper this morning. Did you?" I ask her. Evelyn shakes her head. "If I'm going to be honest, I was afraid to look."

I continue on, "I think we should hire a PR firm to handle the media. The professionals will know how to find a way to use the publicity in a positive way. Think of all the people who will now know about the charity, that didn't know before!" I say, trying my best to spin this disaster into something resembling good news.

"Hmmm," Evelyn begins, "I see why you would want a professional PR firm to take over, but I think we are better served having someone handling the PR who cares about CFF as much as I do. We need someone who appreciates the hard work that has gone into making this Home a reality, and someone who truly understands what is at risk."

I'm already shaking my head before Evelyn can finish her sentence.

"Someone . . . like you, Verity. You should be the face of CFF in this crisis," Evelyn says in a definitive tone.

"Why don't we wait and ask the Board members what they think." I'm not ready to accept the responsibility just yet.

"And speaking of the Board Members, I feel we need to contact all of them and schedule a meeting for later today. Maybe around 2 or 3 p.m.?"

"Yes, that should be our first order of business this morning," Evelyn agrees. "Although, we do need to think about something," Evelyn says, and her whole demeanor becomes very serious. "Detective O'Donnell called me last night and was asking me a lot of questions that really got me thinking of things I didn't want to have to think about. It seems as though he thinks someone connected to CFF has committed this horrendous crime. Of course, I have a hard time believing that, but we must not be naïve."

"Yes, I know. I was thinking the same thing. Detective O'Donnell actually came by my house last night, and his questions about who had access to Jane Street were definitely unsettling, to say the least."

"He came to your house last night?!" Evelyn sounds shocked. "Why?"

"I wasn't answering my phone," I tell her. "He got worried."

"Now *that* is unsettling," Evelyn says.

"I think it's an overreaction, but that doesn't change the fact that members of our Board of Directors may be suspects in this crime. I'm not quite sure how to deal with that. Especially since there is a definite need to meet with everyone today."

"Innocent until proven guilty," Evelyn says. "I have known most of these people for many, many years. I find it almost impossible any of them could, or would kill a young girl. I am confident the evidence will eventually prove their innocence.

Until then, I will continue to treat them all as I always have – like good friends and colleagues."

"I don't think we have any other choice," I agree. "As far as I know, no one on the Board even knew Chloe. The fact that she ended up at Jane Street might just be a terrible coincidence. Maybe the killer knew the building had been empty for a while, thought it would continue to be empty – and would therefore be a good place to hide a body. It's been under construction for so long - I'm sure there are more ways to get into the building aside from the front door with a key. There is no alarm system. Now that I say that, we should definitely have an alarm system installed as soon as possible," I say as I look at Evelyn. She is staring back at me with a blank look and I realize I have been pacing around the room.

"What's wrong?" I ask her.

"I just can't believe we are spending our morning trying to get into the mind of a murderer. This whole situation is just so unbelievable."

"Yes, it is," I agree. "Do you know what is even stranger for me?" I ask. Evelyn shakes her head, looking down at her hands in her lap, inspecting her nails, which are painted a dark red.

"I have been filled with an overwhelming feeling of dread this past week – and I just knew something horrible was about to happen."

"What do you mean?" Evelyn asks looking up at me.

"Remember I told you I had been having nightmares?"

Evelyn nods slowly.

"Well, I'm pretty sure they were about Chloe, and her death. And it wasn't just nightmares, I kept feeling her presence at home, here in the office, in a couple of elevators. I think she is trying to communicate with me. I think she needs my help somehow," I say quietly.

Evelyn stands up, and I'm praying she doesn't just burst out laughing. I'm telling her that a ghost is haunting me – really? I must sound like a crazy person.

"Verity, I know you were there when the body was found, and that must have been very difficult. And I know you have been through traumatic loss in your past . . ." Evelyn says with sincere empathy.

"This is not about my parents," I tell her.

"I don't know what it is, but I'll tell you what it's not – it's not your responsibility. There is a very capable Detective out there whose job it is to find the person that killed this poor girl. And it sounds like he thinks you could also be in danger. Poking around in this case is too risky. And I have to say, the way you speak of this young girl, calling her by her first name, that really worries me, Verity," Evelyn says gravely. "Don't let yourself get too close."

"Evelyn, I appreciate your concern, really I do. But this is something I feel I have to do. I promise to be careful and to not poke too deep," I say lightheartedly, in an attempt to ease her mind. "I don't even know where to start anyway."

Evelyn and I continue our morning trying to return to normalcy. We don't talk about Chloe or the nightmares again – we focus on work. I start to prepare a statement for the press, and email the Board Members about the emergency meeting at 2 p.m. Almost immediately, I hear back from Mitchell, Ryker, David and Chip. They will all be at the meeting, and each of them expressed their concern.

With a pad of paper and a pen, I begin the grueling task of listening to my cell phone and office line voicemails. Ignoring the messages from all the different media outlets, I take notes on all the other calls. Word is out, and the media are foaming at the mouth for the story. Ryker has left a couple of messages on my cell phone, and he sounded pretty worried. I really should have called him back to let him know I'm okay. Once I've listened to all the messages, I start the process of calling people back in order of importance.

Once the messages are returned, I scroll through my emails and respond to the many donors who have written with questions about the CFF Home and the murder. Taking the time to respond to each query, I do my best to reassure people that everything is under control and the project will continue once the police give us the okay to do so. Oh Jane Street, I think sadly, how long will it be before we can begin construction again?

Thinking of construction brings my thoughts to Josh, and the fact that he knew Chloe. Now I know where to begin poking. I call his cell phone and it goes straight to voicemail. I leave a message explaining that I'm calling him to see how he's feeling, and I'm hoping to hear back from him soon. It is a long morning into afternoon of constant phone calls and emails. I decide to wait until I speak with the Board before responding to any media requests. Around 1:30, I begin setting up the conference room, including putting on a pot of coffee and ordering up some sweets from *Baked*, the bakery on the street level of our building. My assumption is that no one got much sleep last night and the caffeine and sugar will be a welcome hit of energy.

Mitchell is the first to arrive a few minutes early. He walks over to Evelyn and gives her a hug, and then, to my surprise, turns and grabs me in a big bear hug as well. I'm not quite sure what to do, so I just stiffly stand there, my arms pinned to my side, and wait for it to end.

"How are you two ladies doing? I've been worried about both of you all day," Mitchell says sweetly.

"We're fine dear. We're two tough broads, you know," Evelyn tells him with a smile.

"Would you like some coffee, Mitchell?" I ask.

"I would love some, thank you, Verity. I would also love one of those toffee cookies – are those from *Baked*?" he asks.

"They are, and, of course." I busy myself getting Mitchell his coffee and cookie and then Ryker, Chip and David arrive almost all at the same time. I don't think David has ever been on time to a meeting, never mind early. But we all know this meeting is unlike any we've ever had.

Ryker walks right over to me and touches my arm, "Verity, I was so glad to get that email from you this morning. When I didn't hear from you yesterday I was so worried. You're lucky I didn't come knocking on your door!"

"I apologize. I had turned my phone off. I wasn't up for conversation last night," I explain.

"The rational side of my brain figured that was the case, but then my imagination almost got the best of me."

"I know. I really am sorry."

"No, I get it. I'm just glad you're okay," Ryker says, and our eyes lock. As I stare into his deep-set blue eyes, a lump forms in my throat. His eyes remind me of the deep part of the Atlantic Ocean – lighter in some areas, but mostly a dark, grayish blue. I wish I didn't ever have to look away. Something has come over me, and in that moment all I want to do is bury myself in his long, strong arms and pretend none of this happened.

Thankfully, Evelyn unknowingly interrupts my daydream by asking Ryker if he'd like some coffee. And just like that, the moment is gone.

"I can get it, Evelyn. Why don't you sit down, I know it's been a long day already," Ryker tells her.

He then turns back to me and asks, "Are you free for dinner tonight? I would love the chance to talk about … well everything."

"I think I should be able to. I guess it depends on how the rest of the afternoon goes," and I unintentionally let out a big sigh.

"I can't even imagine how stressful this must be for you. I think a night out with a handsome, charming guy is just what you need," Ryker says with that amazing smile.

"You know, you're right. Now if only I knew a handsome, charming guy available on such short notice."

"Very funny. I will send my car to pick you up around 7. Should I send it to your house or here?"

"Ugh, probably here. Thanks, Ryker." The day is looking better already.

I sip my coffee and take a minute to gather my thoughts.

This morning, Evelyn and I had agreed that I would run the meeting. She feels she is too close to these men to be able to say some of the things that need to be said. I agree with her. She has known these three, four including Mitchell, a lot longer than I have, and they are like family to her. I can be much more objective. Or so I hope.

"Hi everyone," I begin. "Thank you for being here on such short notice. I know you all have your own fires to put out right now." All the men nod their heads.

"To recap for all of you: the body of a young woman named Chloe Kingston was found concealed in one of the kitchen walls at Jane Street. A member of the construction crew who was in the process of removing the wall discovered it. A Detective O'Donnell is in charge of the investigation. You should all be prepared to be questioned by him, if you haven't been already."

As I'm speaking I look around at the solemn faces looking back at me. Whether done intentionally or not, I see everyone is dressed in dark colors, depicting the mood. I am wearing a black shift dress, black tights and black pumps. However, I'm often in all black. Evelyn, on the other hand, rarely wears black. I notice today she is wearing a black cashmere sweater, a black knee length skirt, sheer black tights and black pointed flats. The men are all in black or navy suits with dark ties. Even Chip has replaced his usual pastel polo with a dark navy sport coat. We are a bleak looking group.

"I am going to be frank with all of you, as there is no way to sugar coat this," I continue. "We are all suspects in this murder. Everyone affiliated with CFF is now a suspect in this murder. Whether that is fair or not, it's the reality. After speaking with Detective O'Donnell last night, I can confirm that we are his focus, including Josh Mesa, the contractor we hired, who I have learned knew Chloe Kingston personally. We are the ones who had access to Jane Street. Evelyn and I ask all of you to cooperate with the police, answer their questions, provide alibis when asked, etc. Please try not to take offense to the questions, and if you get frustrated, please remember the fate of Jane Street, and of CFF, is in your hands."

I'm hoping everyone sitting around this table has realized I am addressing them all with the assumption of their innocence.

Ryker is the first to speak, "Verity, I think I can speak for all of us when I say you have our absolute support and cooperation. Please let us know what we can do to help. Anything at all."

Mitchell, David, and Chip all nod their heads in agreement.

"How do you plan to handle the media?" David asks. "I have a relationship with a great public relations firm, called Specter Group. I'm happy to ask them for assistance in this, if that will help."

"Actually, I was thinking Verity should be the lead on the public relations front," Evelyn interjects. It is the first time she has spoken since the meeting began, and all the men turn their bodies to face her.

"With all due respect to Verity, Evelyn, if there were ever a time to hire a professional PR firm, it's when a dead body is found in your wall. I don't mean to sound callous, but as Verity said, this is not the time to beat around the bush," David says as he absentmindedly rubs his bald head.

"I have to agree with David on this one," Chip chimes in.

"I understand why that would be your first reaction," Evelyn continues, "however, one thing I have been thinking hard about these past two days is trust. And there is no one I trust more than Verity. She is the one person I know who cares as much about what happens to CFF as I do."

"Okay, let's think about this," Ryker says. "Verity does have a law degree, she always chooses her words carefully, and having a young woman showing concern for another young woman could also play well in the media."

"I have to admit, I was not thrilled when Evelyn told me this idea earlier, as I don't feel qualified for such an important job. But perhaps we can compromise. I will speak with someone at Specter Group to brainstorm and get an initial plan together. But then I will be the one speaking directly to the news outlets, making the official statement from CFF, etc." I say looking at Evelyn.

"I think that's a great idea," says Ryker. "Evelyn, David, how do you two feel about that?"

"I would agree to that" David says.

"I think that is fair, thank you," says Evelyn.

"Okay, great. I will contact Specter Group immediately following the end of the meeting," I tell them. "If any of you are contacted by a member of the media, please refer them to me. We have to be very careful right now. As for anything else we can do, unfortunately I'm afraid there isn't much. Right now it is a waiting game as we see what happens with the investigation. Jane Street is closed off as a crime scene. Let's all just pray the Detective can solve this case quickly so that it doesn't drag on in the media. And to all of you, be prepared for a phone call or visit from Detective O'Donnell."

As I'm about to end the meeting, David interjects. "One more thing," he says, looking down at his navy striped tie. "There's something I need to tell everyone."

I look at him quizzically, bracing myself. "What is it, David?"

"I knew Ms. Kingston."

"What?! How?" Mitchell asks, exasperated.

"I knew her too," Ryker says, looking right at me.

I just stand there, trying to mask my surprise. But no one else is trying to hide anything. Their mouths are hanging open in complete and utter shock.

"About six months ago, I had a last minute project and was desperate for help. A friend recommended Chloe . . ." Ryker trails off, his eyes still staring right into mine. I want to look away, but I can't. So this is what it feels like to be punched in the stomach.

"Well, this changes everything," says Mitchell, his voice rising. "We now have a direct connection from CFF to the girl. Two direct connections. Do we include this in the statement we put out? I mean, if the media gets hold of this information by some other means, which they will eventually, then we look like we're hiding something."

"How did you know her, David?" Evelyn asks quietly.

"I mean, I didn't know her well. She decorated our offices when we did the makeover last year. I only met her a couple of times, but I felt I should get it out in the open before you heard it from someone else. I obviously plan to be honest with Detective O'Donnell. He called this morning and asked if he could come speak with me. I put him off until after this meeting, but he'll be coming by my office in an hour or so."

It's as if all the air has been sucked out of the room, and everyone is struggling to breathe.

"Okay. This is not ideal, however, obviously there is nothing David or Ryker can do about the fact that they worked with Chloe in the past. David and Ryker, have either of you had any contact with her recently?" I ask them, praying the answer is no.

"No, I haven't had any contact with her since she finished the office about 4 or 5 months ago," David answers.

"Like I said," Ryker says, "I had her decorate a few apartments about six months ago, and she also was the person who referred Josh Mesa for the contracting job on Jane Street. I had reached out to her for a recommendation when my contractor wasn't available a few weeks ago."

I think I might faint. My head is spinning. Ryker, David and Josh – three direct connections from CFF to a dead woman found buried in the walls at what is now a building owned by CFF.

"Oh my god," Evelyn says in almost a whisper, as she puts her hand up to her mouth. "What are we going to do?"

I sit down for the first time since the meeting started.

"Has anyone else had any contact with Chloe Kingston? Chip? Mitchell?" I ask.

"Not me," says Chip, holding his hands up in defense and shaking his head. "Glad I didn't decide to redecorate recently."

"Of course not," says Mitchell sounding indignant.

"Okay. Well obviously we will have to include in our statement that Chloe had worked for two of our Board Members in the past. And I no longer feel I should be the primary contact for the media. This needs to be handled by a third party – professionals. I'm officially in over my head."

"I have to agree with Verity," Chip says. I think Chip's the only one who can even speak right now, let alone think straight. I've never heard him so serious. "This just got very complicated, and if mishandled, could be devastating."

Everyone is nodding his or her head in agreement, except Evelyn.

"Verity will call Specter Group, but I would still like her to work closely with them," Evelyn says, refusing to give in.

Realizing she's not going to budge on this issue, I change the subject.

"Well then, that was quite a meeting. Now, it's even more important that everyone cooperates with the authorities, and doesn't cooperate with the media. I will give everyone the contact information at Specter Group – please forward all press inquiries to the PR Firm. We all understand what is at stake here."

If the mood at the beginning of the meeting was solemn and bleak, it is now downright morbid. The men quietly file out of the room and Evelyn and I remain. And Ryker.

Sensing his desire to speak with me, Evelyn excuses herself, mumbling something about mountains of work she has to do.

I busy myself by cleaning up the conference table, unable to look up at Ryker who is standing there watching me. For the first time since I've known him, it actually seems like he doesn't know what to say.

"Verity. Please, stop. Look at me," he says.

"I have a lot of work to do, in case you were unaware of the disastrous situation CFF has found itself in," I say sharply, refusing to look at him as I gather napkins and coffee cups and throw them in the garbage.

Ryker is suddenly behind me, and I keep my back to him.

He touches my arm, and speaks softly. "Verity, please. Please agree that you'll still meet me for dinner tonight. Give me a chance to explain."

I whip around and glare at him.

"Explain?! Explain what? The fact that you knew the woman that was found dead in the wall at CFF and you what, forgot to mention that to me?"

"To be fair, I haven't had the chance to talk to you. You didn't call me back last night, remember?" Ryker says defensively, trying to control his temper. "It's not exactly something you leave in a voicemail message. Or would you have preferred I email that to you?" He says with sarcasm dripping from his voice.

"Would you even have told the Board if David didn't do it first?" I ask him.

"To be honest, probably not. My plan was to tell you at dinner. I was hoping to keep it between the two of us," he says sheepishly.

"Seriously, Ryker. You really thought this is something you could keep hidden? You have one of the largest real estate development firms in the city, in the country. And you thought no one is going to make this connection? You are either completely delusional or ridiculously naïve. So which is it?"

"Okay, so maybe it wasn't a good plan. But remember, this all just happened yesterday! I only just found out the woman's body was Chloe's! I'm still trying to process everything and decide what to do. Can you give me a break? Can you just think of the position I'm in for one second?" Ryker pleads.

And then I realize, he's right. It's only been 24 hours since this all happened. I let out a big sigh and look up at him.

"I'm sorry. You're right. I'm stressed out and wound pretty tight right now," I say in a more sympathetic tone. "I have a ton of work to do if I want to get ahead of the media. But, I will still meet you for dinner tonight."

"Thank you," Ryker says with relief. "I will send the car to get you here at the office at 7. I'm really looking forward to being able to talk this all through with you."

An argument can often help release built up tension, and that's just what my squabble with Ryker has done. Now, I'm ready to work. I will fix this mess and get back on track.

Karen McKenna, David's contact from Specter Group PR, is my first phone call. After listening to my brief synopsis of the situation, Karen immediately starts brainstorming and putting a plan together. She knows the story of Chloe's body being found in the wall of a building in the Village (it was in today's paper, ugh), although she was unaware the building was owned by CFF. She seems up to the challenge of managing the damage control for us.

"I will send you the initial statement I was putting together. You can take a look at it and make any changes you feel necessary," I tell her.

"Great. I appreciate that. Is there anything else I should know?" Karen asks.

"Actually, there is," I say slowly. And then I explain everything I know about how David, Ryker and Josh all worked with Chloe.

When I'm finished, Karen says, "Whoa. Okay, this just made things a bit more complicated. But I really appreciate you letting me know from the start. We definitely need to get ahead of this. The connection between the woman and the two Board Members has to come from CFF, not anyone else. That will absolutely have to be in the initial statement."

"Yes, I agree. And now you see our need for professional help with this."

Karen and I talk a little more and then with our to-do lists agreed upon, hang up to get to work. Editing my original statement to include the new information from the meeting, I then email it off to Karen marked "Private. Time Sensitive" in the subject line. With that done, I feel a huge weight lifted off my shoulders.

As I sit at my desk, staring out my window, I continually reflect on my conversation with Detective O'Donnell last night. Does he already know the connection between David and Chloe, or Ryker and Chloe? If he does, he will absolutely be focused on CFF for his suspect pool. I just can't believe David or Ryker could be guilty of killing a young woman and burying her in a wall. I mean, would either one of them even know how to patch up a wall so that no one could tell? Josh would know how to patch up a wall . . . And, what's the motive? Detective O'Donnell seems very capable, but he doesn't know these three men like I do. Afraid the NYPD will spend too much time looking in the wrong places, I know I need to act.

Turning to my computer, I do an Internet search for "Chloe Kingston, New York City". Of course, the first items on the list are media stories about her death. I skim through some of the articles and then scroll down a little more and see her business website, Rex Interiors.

It's a standard website for a small interior designer. The "About Chloe" page on her site displays a photo of a pretty, young woman smiling back at me. She has long blonde hair and brown eyes filled with hope and promise. I learn that she grew up in a small town in Ohio and always wanted to move to New York City and become an interior designer. She felt she was "living her dream" with some of her latest projects that had her working with well-respected developers.

She's probably referring to her work with Ryker. Being able to decorate one of his properties must have been big deal for her professionally. I can't help but wonder why Ryker would hire such an inexperienced designer when he has access to the leaders of the design world in New York City.

Continuing to scroll through her website, I look at some of her before and after photos. She really was good at her job. She would have done well for herself if her life were not cut short. The photos of the Tribeca apartment she decorated for Josh are on the website, and this only further depresses me. A life ended too soon, and my CFF Home for Children lingering on the edge of failure - two casualties of an evil act.

Back to my search results, I find Chloe's Instagram page. Her feed is full of photos of a smiling Chloe at the beach, with girlfriends out to dinner, and one with her arm around a young Asian woman with the caption "Best roommate ever." Her roommate is tagged in the photo as @tinachou. Tina Chou's Instagram page has just what I'm looking for. A photo of Tina in an office with the caption "First day at the new job!" And she tagged @Decker&Bond.

A search for Decker & Bond turns up it's an advertising agency in mid-town. I grab my phone, purse and black leather coat and head out the door, popping my head into Evelyn's office first. "I'm going to run out and get a coffee, can I get you anything?"

"No, thank you, Verity. Take your time and enjoy the fresh air."

"Okay, thank you. Text me if you need anything."

The cab pulls up to a large building on 33rd Street and Lexington Avenue. The whole street level is glass and very modern. In the vast lobby I find the directory and locate Decker & Bond - eighth floor. Looking at the elevators, I'm almost tempted to walk up the eight flights of stairs, but I know it'll take too long. Thankfully I'm on the elevator with about four other people, and it's a quick, uneventful, ride up.

I scan the office of Decker & Bond looking for Tina. In the photo she had streaks of purple in her hair, big hoop earrings and lots of makeup. She should be hard to miss. The office is young and hip, with big meeting areas where people dressed in fitted jeans, t-shirts and Converse sneakers sit around talking. There's a large space with a basketball hoop surrounded by small basketballs all over the floor.

A thirty-something guy in black skinny jeans and a plaid shirt walks over to me.

"Hi, I'm Oliver," he says smiling with his hand outstretched. "Can I help you with something? Do you have a meeting?"

"Hi Oliver," I say shaking his hand, "I'm hoping you can help me. I'm looking for Tina Chou."

His face turns serious. "Is Tina expecting you?" He asks.

"Not exactly. I just wanted to ask her a few questions."

"Look," he says holding his hands up, "if you're with the Press, you can just leave right now. Tina has been through enough in the last couple days, she doesn't need reporters bothering her at work."

"No, look," I tell him. "I'm not a reporter. I knew Chloe Kingston and I just wanted a few minutes to speak with Tina."

At this point I do feel as if I knew Chloe. She's been haunting me for about a week now – that counts.

Oliver tilts his head sideways, and I can see him trying to decide what to do. "I told her not to come into work today. But she said she didn't want to be alone in the apartment with all Chloe's things around her," he says quietly. I guess this must be pretty heavy stuff for an office like this.

"I think she's in the kitchen. You can have 5 minutes, but if you upset her further, you're out. Okay?" He says staring me down.

"Okay. Thank you, I really appreciate it."

Oliver points me toward the kitchen and I immediately see Tina sitting at a table dipping a tea bag in and out of a steaming mug. Her black and purple streaked hair is pulled up in a high bun, and I don't see any jewelry. I walk slowly over to her and touch the back of the seat next to her.

"Do you mind if I sit down, Tina?" I ask her.

She looks up at me with a make-up free face and red-rimmed eyes.

"Um, I guess so. Who are you?" She asks me.

"My name is Verity Townsend."

"How did you know my name?"

"I knew Chloe," I tell her. Tina's eyes grow wide and her bottom lip starts to quiver.

"I don't remember her ever mentioning a Verity. And I think I'd remember that name. Did she decorate your apartment or something?"

"Something like that. Do you mind if I ask you a few questions about her?"

"Okay. But I just told that big Detective everything I know – which isn't much."

"Was Chloe acting weird at all lately? Did anything seem off or different?"

"I'm not sure I understand why you want to know?"

"It's just really important to me. Chloe reached out to me recently and I'm trying to find out why," I say trying not to sound desperate.

"Chloe was always sort of, well, secretive I guess. But she was acting extra strange last week. I can't explain it, but she was home less than usual and then when she was home, she was either staring at her computer or going through some sort of paperwork. I just figured she was just really busy with work."

"Did she say what she was working on?"

"No, she just said it had to do with one of her projects," Tina says as she shrugs her shoulders.

"Did Chloe have a boyfriend?" I ask her. I had noticed on her Instagram page that there wasn't one photo with a guy.

"Well, that's what's weird. She was seeing someone, but she said she couldn't tell me who it was yet. She said she should be able to tell me soon. But we never got that far," and Tina's lower lip begins to quiver again.

"Do you know anything about this guy? Did she ever slip up on a name, or nickname? Something about his age or his looks? Anything?"

"I know he was older than us and, I'm not sure I should say this, because I'm not totally positive, but I think he was married."

"Really? What makes you think that?" I ask.

"I overheard her on her cell phone once. She was asking the person, I'm assuming it was him, she was asking him how much longer she had to wait for him to leave her. I realized that was probably why she couldn't tell me his name. Other than that, I don't know anything about him."

"That's helpful, Tina. I know this is hard, so thank you for speaking with me." I grab a napkin and pull a pen out of my bag. I write my name and cell phone number on the napkin and hand it to her.

"Please call me if you think of anything else. You never know what might help find who did this to Chloe. And if you ever need anything, someone to talk to . . . please don't hesitate to contact me."

On my cab ride back down to the CFF office, I keep going over and over everything Tina told me. Chloe was reserved, had an older, secret boyfriend that was possibly married, and was working on something recently that she wouldn't tell Tina about. Whew - that's a lot of good information. On the other hand, it creates a lot more questions.

The ringing of my phone interrupts my thoughts. I look down at my phone screen and see that it's Tessa. This is the third time she's called since yesterday. I can't put off the conversation any longer.

"Hey, Tessa," I answer casually.

"Hey Tessa? Seriously? Where have you been? Are you okay? Or are you dead somewhere buried in a wall? I'm freaking out! Oh my god, Verity! What the heck is going on?!"

This is why I hadn't called Tessa back yet.

"I'm sorry, it's been crazy. I'm totally fine. Obviously there's a lot going on at work . . ." I trail off.

"When can I see you? We need to talk. What are you doing tonight?" Tessa asks.

"I actually have dinner plans tonight. How about we grab coffee in the morning?"

"Okay, that sounds good. What time?"

"Let's meet at Roast at 9."

"Okay, see you tomorrow. And Verity, please be careful."

By the time I arrive back at CFF I am determined to find out the identity of Chloe's mysterious boyfriend. I re-read the pages on Chloe's website, study the photos of offices and apartments she had designed, and just as I am about to look through her Instagram photos again, my phone dings – I have a text: *I'm in the car downstairs. Ready?*

Wow, 7 p.m. came quick today. I promise myself I'll look through the Instagram photos later tonight, but now, dinner with Ryker.

When I get downstairs Ryker is leaning on his car, in an expertly tailored pinstripe suit. His normally perfectly coifed hair is falling into his face a little, making him look young, and dare I say, vulnerable. I see the exhaustion in his face as he reads something on his cell phone.

"Hey there," I say as I walk up to him.

"Why, hello," he smiles at me, and puts his phone down. "Was your day as great as mine?" He asks sarcastically.

I can't help but laugh. Despite my annoyance with him earlier today, I am glad I decided to meet him.

"Hop in, I have a great little spot I want to take you to down in SoHo."

We chat about little things as we head downtown. I think we're both happy to distract each other from all that's going on, if only for a few minutes.

The car stops in front of a little Japanese restaurant. Man, he knows me well.

"I remember you mentioning once that you liked sushi," he says.

"I do. Very much," I reply.

We get a small table for two by the front window. Ryker orders us a bottle of white wine. "Does that sound okay to you?" He asks.

'Yes, that sounds great. And why don't you let me order the food," I say challenging the control freak in him.

"Oh, I see. Okay, I can do that. I've had all the popular sushi rolls, like California rolls . . ."

"I'm going to stop you right there," I interrupt him. "No California rolls allowed at my sushi table. Get ready to have your mind blown."

I order some seaweed salad, edamame and gyoza's to start, and an array of sashimi, sushi and hand rolls. When I finish ordering, I notice Ryker is looking at me with what I can only describe as fear. I can't help but laugh.

"What is so funny?" He asks, beginning to laugh himself.

"Your face. You look so scared! I didn't think *the* Ryker Rensselaer was afraid of anything!" I tease him.

"Well, considering I have no idea what you just ordered -- I will admit to a fear of the unknown. Seaweed? Gyo-what? Yup, I'm afraid."

"You will be pleasantly surprised. I promise. I haven't been out to eat in SoHo in a while. Thank you - I really needed this." I say looking across the small table at him.

"It is always my pleasure. Seriously."

I look down shyly, and quickly change the subject. "I hate to do this, but I feel we do need to talk about Chloe." Ryker nods his head, acknowledging this conversation needs to happen.

"One thing I'm confused about -- why would Ryker Realty, arguably the most successful real estate development firm in New York, why would you hire such an inexperienced designer for one of your projects?" I ask him. "Any and every designer in the city would be dying to work with you."

"You have to understand, Verity. I have so many deals occurring simultaneously, it can be hard to keep track of what phase of the process I am in with each one. My assistant, Irene, who is absolutely amazing, was out sick with the flu for almost an entire week. There was a building I had purchased months prior, and had renovated it – turned it into multiple apartments. A young realtor on my team called me in a panic that he had buyers lined up for the apartments, and he was afraid if he waited much longer to show them a finished product, he would lose them. So, I told him to stage one of the apartments, and show all the buyers that one, as the model. With Irene out sick, I didn't have time to go through my list of designers and find one available immediately. And by immediately, I mean – I needed them to go to the building that day. This young realtor said he had a friend that staged homes all the time; she was really good, etc. So, I told him, if he trusted her, to go ahead and hire her. But if the place looked like something straight out of a Pottery Barn catalogue, it was on him." Ryker pauses and takes a sip of his wine.

"So, how did Chloe do?" I ask him.

"I was impressed, actually. I went to check up on the progress, and got to speak with her quite a bit. She was a sweet girl. I could tell she was really nervous, but excited for the opportunity. I offered her some guidance and explained exactly what we wanted the space to look like, and she did a good job. She definitely had a lot of potential," Ryker says this last sentence quietly.

"But, then you never used her again?"

"No, I never got the chance to," he says with sadness in his voice. "And not by any fault of her own – I just have a few designers that I have so much trust in, I don't even have to check in on them. I can tell them the feel I want to create in a space, and I know they will deliver exactly what I'm looking for. When time is of the essence, which it always is in real estate, it's just easier to go with someone I completely know and trust."

"I understand that – and thank you for explaining this all to me. I know it's not a fun topic of conversation for a night out."

"It's okay. I wanted to tell you everything. Do you know why I took you here?" Ryker asks, seamlessly transitioning out of talk about Chloe. "Aside from your love of sushi – it's this location. Do you see that clothing store at the corner of Spring and Greene?" he says, pointing across the street.

I nod my head.

"You know I am a big history buff, especially when it comes to New York City's history. And you see, buried in the walls of that building is an old brick well. Now, you are aware of my obsession with all things Alexander Hamilton, right? Well, he has a connection to this well. In December of 1799, a young woman named Gulielma Sands, or Elma as she was more commonly called, was set to elope with her lover, a man named Levi Weeks. Levi Weeks was living in the same boarding house as Elma, but his brother, Ezra Weeks, was powerful and wealthy. And rumor has it that Ezra did not approve of Elma."

As Ryker is talking, our food begins to get served. I dig into the seaweed salad and edamame, sipping my wine – delighted to escape my own thoughts for a little while.

Ryker is so engrossed in his story he doesn't realize that he too is enjoying seaweed and gyoza. I'll tell him later.

"Now, Elma tells another housemate that she and Levi are to have a secret meeting to elope one night. Poor Elma is never heard from again. Two days later, young Elma's body is found at the bottom of the Manhattan Well. Some people as far as a half-mile away claim to have seen Elma riding on a sleigh with a man, some say two men. Levi Weeks is arrested for the murder."

I'm listening intently to Ryker's story, and trying to ignore the flashes from my nightmares - Chloe's dusty head of hair hanging out of the wall, her large, unblinking eyes staring out at me from under water, and that bloated hand reaching for me. A woman being chased, and then drowned. "So, she was found in a well in that building right over there?" I manage to get out.

Ryker nods his head as he takes a bite of raw tuna.

"But wait, you said this was about Alexander Hamilton? How does he fit in to this?"

"Well, the arrest of Levi Weeks sparks the first ever murder trial in the United States. Ezra Weeks, the wealthy, connected older brother of Levi, hires the two best attorneys in all of New York City: Alexander Hamilton and Aaron Burr." Ryker pauses for effect and raises his eyebrows, waiting for my response.

"Wow, I had no idea! So Alexander Hamilton and Aaron Burr were on the same side only a short time before Burr kills Hamilton in a duel?!"

"That's right. Crazy, huh?"

"And whatever happened with Levi Weeks? Was he found guilty of murdering Elma Sands?" I ask, captivated by the story.

"After a two day trial, the jury deliberated for five minutes, and acquitted Levi Weeks. Although the jury was convinced Levi was innocent, public opinion was starkly divided. Many people thought Levi got away with murder. But lots of other people thought Ezra was guilty. I guess we'll never know."

"This is fascinating. I can't believe I didn't know this!" I tell him.

"And better yet, some people claim to have seen the ghost of Elma Sands around SoHo," Ryker says with a smirk.

"I believe it," I say quietly as I look down, squeezing an eel roll with my chopsticks.

"Are you telling me that Verity Townsend, one of the most practical women I know, believes in ghosts?!" Ryker says, mocking me.

"I am a complicated woman," I tell him, "full of surprises." And I offer him a devilish smile.

"I can't, won't, argue with that," Ryker says and holds up his wine glass in a toast. "Cheers to you, Verity, and all your complicated surprises."

Chapter 15

Ryker's car drops me off at my house around 10:30. I have to admit, the cozy Japanese restaurant, the wine, Ryker's attention and stimulating conversation, and I'm floating through the door. Despite all the horror that has happened in the past 2 days, tonight has me with a permanent smile, and dare I say, giddy.

Once inside my quiet, dark house, I kick off my heels, hang my coat in the closet and head into the kitchen. I'm still reeling from dinner, and know I won't be able to fall asleep just yet. I bring my laptop over to the couch and plan to do some more research on Chloe.

Back on Chloe's Instagram page, I start to go through each photo, one at a time. There are lots of photos of her finished designs, pictures with friends out to dinner, or out at a club. In one photo I recognize the club she's at as Ice – I'll have to ask Ryker if he ever saw her there. I also meant to ask Ryker if he has spoken to Josh Mesa. I've been meaning to call him and see how he's doing. I'll have to do that tomorrow.

One photo seems to stand out from the rest - it's Chloe by herself in her pajamas, drinking coffee. She looks adorable with messy hair, smudged mascara, a navy sheet and striped duvet tousled around her – so happy and sweet. I am suddenly struck with an overwhelming feeling of love – of painful, yearning, lost love. The feeling is so strong tears spring to my eyes and my heart aches inside my chest. I turn my laptop off. It's time to call it a night.

She reaches down and grabs her heavy skirt from both sides, hoisting it up, the back of it dragging along the dirt road. As she runs, her corset digs into her back, and her long blonde hair falls out of its bun and around her face. Her left stocking slips down her leg – the garter ribbon has come untied. But she pushes all this out of her mind and focuses on running as fast as she can. She's got to find him. The sign for Jane Street hangs at the intersection, and turning to look down the street, she sees a small group of men. With relief, she slows down to a walk. As she gets closer, she sees there are two separate groups of men facing each other. She sees a few men in their breeches and high socks, some wearing coats with tails. One man in particular has a powdered wig and top hat – that's him!

A sudden bang echoes through the streets. And then another. The man in the wig and top hat collapses to the ground, holding his stomach. Some of the men scatter, a few race to the fallen man's side. The blonde girl rushes to see who has been shot, but deep down she already knows. "Noooo," the word comes out like a moan. As she gets closer, she realizes she's right. Alexander Hamilton is down and blood is starting to pool under his limp body. A doctor is yelling orders at people in a panic, "Bring him to Bayard's!"

But the Bayard house is not where it's supposed to be – it's not the brick house on the south side of the street. Everyone is heading to a large field on the corner of the north side of the street. There is a big house set far back on the land. Confused, she starts to yell at the men -- they're going the wrong way! No one can hear her.

Then her body stiffens in fear. She hears heavy breathing behind her - she knows she's in danger. He's caught up to her. She starts running again, this time she turns down an alley. He's right on her heels. She turns around to face him, stumbling backward – and he's on her. The man grabs her from her underarms and drags her over to a brick well, as she kicks and screams. He hoists her up and over the top of the well, but her legs are still hanging out. He then grabs her legs and throws them over too. And she's gone.

It's 7:30 a.m. when I wake up. Dragging myself out of bed, I get dressed in some running gear and head outside to hit the streets. It's light out already and the sidewalks are busier than I'm used to. That's what I get for waking up so late. I make a game out of weaving in and out of pedestrians and try to stay patient at crosswalks. The truth is, I'm very distracted this morning - unable to shake last night's strange dream. Chloe and Alexander Hamilton? The Bayard Mansion? And then watching Chloe get murdered and tossed down a well. What does it all mean? Before I know it, I am back at my stoop. Unlike most post-runs, today there is no clear head. But, it's time to get showered and dressed to go meet Tessa.

Despite my odd morning, I arrive at Roast right at 9 a.m., and quite to my surprise, Tessa is already waiting for me. I see her at a small table by the fireplace, her blonde curls pulled back from her face. She's dressed in a cream loose, flowy dress that hits about . . . let's just say it *just* covers her behind. It's *very* short. And she has on suede thigh-high boots the color of rich cognac, with about a 3" block heel. Giant hoop earrings hang from her ears. She's sitting with her legs crossed, staring at her iPhone. A furrowed brow and a worried expression have replaced Tessa's typically jubilant face. She can usually dress casually for her job as the Creative Assistant for Posh Magazine.

The magazine expects their employees to look current and stylish, but their idea of professional is different than most.

I walk over to her before I order my coffee, and she doesn't notice me until I sit down right across from her. "You know you'll get wrinkles if you keep staring at your phone like that," I say to her.

Tessa's head pops up at the sound of my voice. "Oh my, Verity! Thank god you're okay!" and she gets up and jumps across the table to wrap me in a giant hug, about a dozen bracelets jangle as she moves.

"What the heck is going on?" She starts to yell, but then brings it down to a whisper when she sees me putting my finger to my lips to shush her.

"I mean seriously V, did you really find a body in the new CFF building?" She whisper yells.

"Let's order first. What can I get you?" I ask her.

"Vanilla latte and a chocolate croissant, please."

Up at the counter, I say hello to Frank, the owner, and order my Americano, Tessa's latte, a chocolate croissant and a veggie egg-white omelet with no cheese. I bring the coffees back to our table, and notice that Tessa is just staring at me, blue eyes wide and curious.

"Start from the beginning," she tells me.

I start from the day Chloe's body was discovered and tell her everything I can think of – from the way Chloe's body looked (Tessa, of course, wants all the gory details). I tell her how Josh Mesa, the head contractor, knew Chloe. As I'm talking, Frank brings us our food. Tessa listens intently as I talk about how Detective O'Donnell showed up at my house, all the emails from the media, and the Board meeting where Ryker and David admitted to knowing Chloe.

"And here we are. You're all caught up. As you can see, it's been an insane two days."

"So you had never heard from Chloe before you saw her dead body?" Tessa asks.

"Well, that's not totally true," I say looking down at my coffee.

"What do you mean?" Tessa asks.

"Well, I had never met her before in person . . ." I trail off.

"But what, you talked to her on the phone? Email? Text? What?" Tessa asks, exasperated.

"You're probably going to think I'm crazy. But, I've been having these dreams – nightmares really."

"Haven't you always had nightmares? I mean, since your parents died?" Tessa asks quietly.

"Well yes, but they did go away for awhile. And these new nightmares were . . . from Chloe. She was in my dreams – and she's been trying to tell me things. I think she wants me to help find her killer."

"Okayyyyy. So, you see dead people?" Tessa says with a small smile, quoting an old movie from the 90's.

"Ha. Very funny, Tessa. But I'm serious. The dreams are scary – there is a man chasing me and I know he's going to kill me. But they're confusing—sometimes I see a man throw a woman down a well, and it's like 200 years ago. And a few times I've felt a force holding me under water, and I can actually feel what it's like to drown." This last thought makes me shudder, but I can't stop talking.

"And I smell this sweet floral smell in almost all the nightmares. I have also smelled it at my office, and in a few elevators, where I swear Chloe's spirit was there with me. Once I smelled it in the kitchen at Jane Street, which is where Chloe's body was found."

Stopping to take a breath, I look across at Tessa and I can't tell if she's confused or concerned. But I just keep talking.

"In last night's dream – I watched the duel where Alexander Hamilton is shot. They are taking his body to his friend's house, William Bayard, where Hamilton actually died in real life. Except, they're going the wrong way. I know the Bayard mansion; it's across the street from the new CFF home on Jane Street. But in the dream they take him to where the CFF house is now. But there's no building there. It's a field with a big mansion set really far back."

I pause, "You think I'm crazy."

"No, I don't think you're crazy. I totally believe in ghosts and signs from the other side – all that stuff. I mean, you were practically haunted by your parents for years after they died. But I do have a few questions. I have no idea how Alexander Hamilton fits into this whole thing, or Bayard or whoever. But why would this Chloe come to you? It makes me think you are somehow connected to the killer, which is . . . terrifying," Tessa's eyes are wide as I see her going through it all in her head.

"Let's break this down," she says. "There's a well from 200 years ago. That can't be where she was killed, because wells like that don't exist anymore. So, what could that mean?"

"Oh my god," I interrupt her, "Elma Sands."

"Elma who?" Tessa asks.

"Elma Sands. She was a young woman murdered in like 1800 or something, her body was found in a well. A well here in New York City – in SoHo," my voice is getting higher. "And, Alexander Hamilton was the attorney that got her alleged accuser acquitted. How did I not connect this? Chloe drowned."

"Wait," says Tessa, "How do you know about this Elma?"

"Well, Ryker told me . . ." And my voice trails off.

"Is she trying to tell you something about Ryker? About how they knew each other?" Tessa asks quietly.

"I don't know. But I need to look into this more. I have a few ideas."

"Verity, be careful," Tessa says with concern. "You have no idea what you might be getting yourself into. This could be seriously dangerous. Like, seriously."

My head is spinning as I grab a cab down to CFF. Hamilton, Bayard, Elma, Chloe, Jane Street . . . Ryker? It has to all be connected. And I will find out how – not only to help Chloe and bring her killer to justice, but to stop the nightmares.

My cell phone rings and I see it's an unknown New York number.

"Hello, this is Verity."

"Ms. Townsend, I'm so glad I reached you. This is Detective O'Donnell. I have a couple more questions to ask you if you can spare some time."

The sound of Detective O'Donnell's deep voice makes my heart begin to race. I don't know why I'm so nervous; I certainly have nothing to hide.

"I can talk now, but I only have a few minutes," I tell him, giving myself an out.

"No problem, this shouldn't take long. "When was the first time you saw Chloe Kingston?"

"I think I told you this already. The first time I saw her was when her body was discovered at the CFF building on Jane Street," I say impatiently.

"Okay. Were you aware that your associates David Cohen and Ryker Rensselaer both knew the victim prior to her death?"

"I was just made aware of this yesterday," I say without hesitation.

"And, correct me if I'm wrong, but didn't you say Mr. Cohen was trying to stall the start to the construction, claiming something was wrong with his expediter?"

"Excuse me, Detective, but please don't put words into my mouth. I definitely did not say David was 'stalling' the construction. If I remember correctly, I simply stated that David thought his expediter might not be able to self-certify the permit as quickly as we wanted them to. However, in the end, they both came through." Now I'm getting worked up.

"Okay. Thank you for clarifying that. Were you also aware that your contractor, Joshua Mesa, worked with the victim frequently before she was murdered?"

"You already told me they knew each other before Chloe was drowned, but I am unaware to what extent."

"Ms. Townsend, how did you know the victim was drowned? We have not released this information to the public."

Ugh. I walked right into that one. Can I tell him I had a dream about it? He'll have me committed.

"Well, I'm just guessing actually. I didn't see any blood on her, and she was a little blue and swollen looking. Why, am I right?"

I'm so glad the Detective can't see my face right now, because it's bright red and I'm starting to sweat - clear signs of a liar.

"Well, aren't you quite the detective, Ms. Townsend. Maybe you should have my job," he says, but it's not a compliment. He's too smart to just let this go.

"People always tell me I have a real eye for the details," I say lightheartedly. "You know what, I just got to a meeting, I really have to go."

"Okay then. And if you think of any other *details* you may not have mentioned, you be sure and give me a call, okay?"

"Of course. Absolutely. Bye now," I say quickly, and hang up.

Well that was a disaster. In the future I'll have to remember not to answer the phone when an unidentified number is displayed on the screen.

Chapter 16

Pushing the conversation with Detective O'Donnell out of my mind, I spend the morning focused on work - following up with emails, and talking with Karen from Specter Group. The reaction from our initial statement has been relatively positive. No one is pointing fingers directly at CFF. Well, not yet anyway. Karen definitely used her connections to get our message portrayed in a favorable light, playing CFF as another victim in this horrible crime - a children's charity trying to open a home for orphans, and then a poor young woman found dead on the new property. It was mentioned that the building had only been CFF's for a couple days. And then somewhere in the middle of the statement it mentions that Chloe was a young interior designer who had done work with many companies around New York City, including Ryker Realty and Hancock, Metz & Cohen. It really was a work of art.

With work caught up, there are a few things I need to get done. Josh Mesa -- why have you been avoiding my calls? Even if you're grieving, you are still a professional and need to deal with your work.

I dial Josh's cell phone number and after about five rings, when I'm about ready to hang up, I hear a rushed "Hello?" as if he's out of breath.

"Josh, is that you?"

"Ah, yes, this is Josh," and I hear some strange shuffling noises on the line.

"Josh, this is Verity. Is everything okay?"

"Oh, Verity. Yes. Yes, everything is okay. I'm just doing a million things, you know me. How are you?"

"I'm fine. Josh, I've called you quite a few times and I haven't heard back. Detective O'Donnell told me you worked with Chloe . . . how are you dealing with everything?"

"I'm sorry I haven't returned your calls. I've been a little out of it the past few days, to be honest. It was quite a blow, as you can imagine."

"Yeah, I understand. I'm glad to hear you're feeling better."

"Yes, I am. And please, Verity, please know that as soon as the building is cleared and ready to go, my crew will be ready too. I'm still your guy."

"Thanks, that's great to hear. Josh, you know me well enough already – I go straight to the point. Do you mind if I ask you a few questions about Chloe?

"Of course not. What is it you'd like to know?"

"When did you two meet?

"We met a few years ago. I was called in to give a quote on renovating a bathroom in an apartment in Queens and Chloe was there doing the design for the client. She was really smart, and I could tell she was talented. From that point forward we started collaborating on projects together."

"Do you know if she was seeing anyone?"

"Jeez, Verity, you sound like that detective. No, I didn't know anything about her personal life. Our relationship was strictly professional."

"So Detective O'Donnell has contacted you?"

"Yeah, he was here last night. Not the friendliest guy, is he? He made me doubt everything I said," Josh says with a nervous laugh.

"I think I know what you mean. Anyway, I will keep you posted on anything going on with Jane Street. Hopefully none of your crew members are too spooked to come back."

"No, my guys are tough. Although, this is definitely not your typical construction issue."

"No, it's not. And one more thing, Josh - the media might find out you were there when the body was found, or that you were the contractor hired to renovate Jane Street. You should prepare yourself for this type of questioning. Reporters will absolutely be calling you and asking you all sorts of things." Josh hasn't said a word, so I continue, "For the sake of your reputation and the reputation of CFF, please forward all media inquiries to the PR Firm we've hired. It's a firm called Specter Group, and our point person is a woman named Karen McKenna. We need to have a united front on this, and keep the message consistent."

"Right . . . of course. Whatever you think is best," Josh says, sounding blindsided.

"Thank you, Josh. And if you have any other questions or problems, please don't hesitate to call me."

The strange conversation with Josh has me feeling a little uneasy about him. But, for now, I need to attack the next item on my to-do list: The Bayard Mansion. Chloe is pointing me to the Bayard Mansion for some reason, and I'm determined to find out why. Researching William Bayard, I discover he was a prominent NYC banker. He was married to Elizabeth Bayard and together they had seven children. He, of course, is most famous for being close friends with Alexander Hamilton. There are lots of mentions that his home, what is today's 82 Jane Street, is the location of Hamilton's death.

I type "Bayard mansion Jane Street" into the search engine. Scrolling a few searches down I see an old *NY Times* article written by a Michael Pollak, called: "The Plaque at 82 Jane Street is False." It reads:

> *"According to Terry Miller and his 1990 book "Greenwich Village and How it Got That Way," the apartment house with the plaque on the south side of Jane Street, dates from 1886, Mr. Miller wrote. The problem, Mr. Miller wrote is that the Bayard House never stood there. A map drawn in 1767 places William Bayard's house below the present Gansevoort Street. The house was on the North side of Jane Street, close to and possibly in the path of current day Horatio Street, which wasn't mapped until 1817.*

> *But this hardly mattered to the 1936 owner of 82 Jane Street, who installed this plaque thereby slipping his building into a half a century's worth of books about the Village, Miller wrote.*

As I read this, my heart begins to pound. Quickly, I pull up a map of Greenwich Village on my screen to confirm what I already know. My pulse quickens as my mind begins to realize what this means. As I look at Horatio Street and Jane Street on the map, it becomes evident -- the Bayard House was on the north side of Jane Street and sat far back on the road. This means, 76 Jane Street is the actual location of what was the old Bayard House. The new CFF home stands on the sacred ground where Alexander Hamilton took his last breath. And now, another young person has lost their life much too soon on the same plot of land.

What is Chloe's connection to Jane Street? Is she using Hamilton's death to draw parallels to her own? But he was shot, and Chloe was drowned. Was she killed at Jane Street? If so, why was she there to begin with? Or was she killed somewhere else and just buried at Jane Street? I still am not any closer to figuring out what happened to her.

As I'm thinking this, as if by divine intervention, my phone "dings" with a text. I look, and it's from Tina Chou: *Verity, we need to talk. Can you come to my apartment?*

Chapter 17

Grabbing my handbag, I practically run out of my office. I am in such a hurry I don't even remember to tell Evelyn I'm leaving. I'll just have to text her from the cab. Tina's apartment (Chloe's former apartment) is on the Upper East Side of Manhattan. And it is waaay east, which because it's far from any subway line ,is where you can find the real deals in the city. However, with the recent opening of the 2nd Avenue subway, all those properties that used to be in no-man's-land will now be more valuable.

The apartment is in a small brick building with six floors, and Tina lives on the fifth floor. At the intercom system outside the front door to the building, I find "Kingston/Chou" and hit the buzzer.

"Hello?" Tina says quietly.

"Tina? It's Verity. Want to buzz me up?"

"Yeah, just a minute," she says and then I hear the click as the door unlocks followed by a loud buzzing sound. Pulling the heavy door open, I walk into the small lobby area. Aside from a wall of mailboxes, there isn't much to see. No doorman – and no elevator. Ugh.

I head over to the stairs and begin the climb. This was not the day to wear 4" heels. But I use the time to go over some questions I want to ask Tina, and my head is so full I reach the fifth floor landing quickly. But now I'm sweating and need to take off my coat.

In front of apartment 5C, I hear soft music through the door. I give a pretty loud knock to be sure she can hear me. Tina opens the door halfway, and she looks even younger than she did the first time I met her. Her hair is pulled up in a high bun, almost on top of her head. She has no makeup on, and is wearing a white tank top, gray fitted sweatpants and fuzzy bunny slippers. She looks 12 years old, although she's probably only a few years younger than me.

Once she confirms it's me, she opens the door all the way and invites me in.

"Do you want some coffee or something?" Tina asks.

"No thank you, I'm fine. How are you holding up?" I ask her.

"I'm okay. I still can't believe this is happening. I couldn't go into work today. I was hoping work would be a distraction, but honestly, I was the distraction. No one knew what to do or say around me. I think I made them all uncomfortable."

"I understand. I think it's a good thing you're staying home for a little while. You've got to give yourself some time." I tell her as I follow her over to the tiny round table set up between their kitchen and their couch, which I guess would be considered their dining room. But since this one room, which holds the kitchen, dining room and living room is only about 400 square feet; it's hard to say. There is a bedroom off each side of the main room, and one bedroom door is open and one is closed. I'm guessing behind that closed door hides what was once Chloe's bedroom. I'm sure that's Tina's way of trying to avoid thinking about Chloe. I can't say I blame her.

Once we sit down, I ask Tina, "Why'd you ask me to come here today, Tina? Has something happened?" As I've mentioned, I am not one to beat around the bush.

"Well, nothing new has really happened, but there are a few things I wanted to tell you. The police have been here, of course, and they went through Chloe's bedroom," as she says this she nods slightly toward the room with the closed door. "And they took a lot of things with them and asked me questions, for what seemed like hours, it's all such a blur." As she talks, Tina holds her coffee mug tight and her dark brown eyes are steady and serious.

"Okay. I understand."

"Well, I realize that, first of all, they never found Chloe's laptop or her phone. They weren't in her room or anywhere else in the apartment."

"Did the police know they should be looking for her laptop and phone?" I ask.

"Yes. I figured it was the case since they already searched her office, then searched her room, and said there was no sign of any type of computer. They asked me if Chloe had a laptop or tablet or something. I told them she had a laptop that basically never left her side. But I wanted to tell you this too. I don't know why, I just thought it might help. "

"That does help, Tina. Thank you. Was there something else?" I really hope so, I think to myself. I better not have just come halfway across the city and walked up five flights of stairs in 4" heels to be told something that could have been easily relayed over the phone.

"Yes. I kept seeing Chloe with the same folder constantly those last few weeks. It was just a blue, regular, two-pocket folder. And well, this is really why I wanted you to come - the police didn't take it. They glanced through it, but I still saw it there in her room after they left."

"Where is it now?" I asked, starting to get my hopes up.

"It's still in her room. I can't go in there."

"Do you mind if I go in Chloe's room?" I ask as gently as possible.

"No. Please, go ahead. That's why I didn't just call you on the phone, I wanted you to come here so you could go in her room to get it."

"Thank you so much, Tina. Why don't you just stay here, and I'll go look in her room for the folder."

Chloe's room is very feminine with light gray walls, and light pink and turquoise accents all around. There is a queen-sized bed, with a medium gray tufted headboard, white sheets, a pale pink duvet and about a million pillows. She has a white dresser with a gold-framed mirror above it, and a white desk under the window. A gray tufted armchair, which matches the headboard, is tucked under the desk. The whole room is in slight disarray, from the police going through everything, but that is not what's bothering me. Something is not right.

The bed.

I think back to the photo from Chloe's Instagram page. It was the photo I was staring at that brought tears to my eyes - the photo of Chloe sitting on her bed, smiling, with navy and striped bedding all around her. That's not her bed she's sitting on. It must be her boyfriend's bed. Now we're getting somewhere.

Over on the ornate white desk, I see the blue folder Tina was talking about. I anxiously open it up, thinking I'm going to discover the answers to all my questions, and am so disappointed when I see that the folder is empty. I was really hoping to find out what Chloe was researching the last few weeks of her life, but if there was anything important in that folder, the police took it.

I pick the folder up in one last-ditch effort to find a clue, and look deep into each pocket. I see something. It looks like a photo turned around, so the back of it is facing out. The back of the photo is white, as is the inside of the folder, so I can see how the police missed it.

Turning the photo around, my mouth falls open -- I can hardly believe my eyes. It's the photo of Chloe sitting on the navy striped bed – but her Instagram photo must have been cropped. This photo has Chloe smiling at the camera, sitting next to her boyfriend - a half-dressed Johnny Mesa.

Tucking the photo into my purse, I leave Chloe's room, and say a quick good-bye to Tina. Explaining the blue folder was empty; I thank her, and try to hide my desire to quickly leave.

Tina slumps a little in disappointment. But I tell her not to worry, we will figure this whole thing out. Honestly, I don't even know what I said; I am so distracted by the face of Johnny Mesa running through my head. His devilish, charming smile and the way he shook my hand for just a little too long. Wait, if he's the boyfriend, then that means he's married? *He's* married? Whoa. I need to get out of this apartment and do some research on Mr. Mesa.

cab ride back to my office in mid-town is a blur. I

ve I have discovered who Chloe's secret boyfriend was.

t believe that boyfriend is Johnny Mesa. So, what's my next step? Do I confront him? On the phone or in person? Definitely in person. I want to see his face when I tell him I know his dirty little secret.

My thoughts are interrupted by the ding of my phone - I have a text message. I look at my phone and it's from Tessa: *How are you? I'm worried about you.*

I quickly text her back: *I'm good. Making progress* ☺

Tessa's text back is real subtle: *BE CAREFUL. Someone you talk to today could be a murderer!!!*

I know. I'm fine. Chill out. Will call you later. I respond. She's so dramatic.

But then I realize, if Johnny is the boyfriend, and he's married, could he have killed Chloe in a crime of passion? Did Chloe want to tell his wife about them? Was she pressuring too much for him to leave his wife? I think back to what Tina told me about the conversation she overheard – Chloe asking, who we now know is Johnny, how much longer she had to wait for him to leave his wife. And Chloe also worked for them, quite a bit. That would be really awkward if Johnny broke it off with Chloe and then had to continue to work with her. Did Josh know they were seeing each other? Is this what Josh and Johnny were arguing about that time I walked in on them at Jane Street? There are so many unanswered questions. But the timing of that argument, would Chloe still have been alive?

At my office, I say a quick hello to Evelyn and sit at my computer. My emails will have to wait. An Internet search for

"John Mesa" doesn't result in very much. He doesn't seem to have much going on in the social media realm. I guess people who cheat on their spouses are a little too secretive to be "checking in" to restaurants or hotels. They don't want anyone knowing where they are or who they're with. Gross.

He is mentioned in some articles with Josh, and he's got a page about his business on Josh's website. The page about him on Josh's website is mostly about his work experience. There are links to other pages showing photos of carpentry work he has done – kitchen cabinets, impressive built-ins in dens and family rooms. He really is talented. And then at the very bottom of the page about him, it says, "Johnny lives in New York City with his beautiful wife, Melissa."

I'm even more sure I'm right. He is married. He was cheating on his wife with Chloe. I will need to meet Johnny in a public place. I don't want to be alone with him. The website lists a contact number for Johnny. Not wasting any time to think and talk myself out of it, I make the call. Here goes nothing.

The phone rings quite a few times - Why don't these Mesa men answer their phone? Just when I'm about ready to hang up, I hear a groggy, "Hello?"

"Hi, I'm looking for Johnny?" I say.

"Ahh, this is Johnny. How can I help you?" he says, sounding a little more normal.

"This is Verity Townsend, we met once. I'm with the CFF Home," I say, purposely not mentioning Jane Street.

"Oh right, Verity, of course. What can I do for you, Verity?"

"I'm sorry, did I wake you?"

I'm fine. It's just been a crazy week, that's all. Well,
' He says, and his voice trails off.

es, I know. I'm not sure what your day looks like, but I
was hoping to meet with you later."

I can sense his hesitation. "It's work related. You'd really
be doing me a favor."

"Um, I guess I could do that. What time were you
thinking?"

"I was thinking later, around 5. I promise I won't take up
too much of your time.

"Sure, that's fine."

"I will text you the location. Thanks so much Johnny. I will
see you later."

"I'll see you later," he says, sounding less than happy.

Denery's Pub is a local joint in SoHo that is always busy at
happy hour. Arriving 15 minutes early to be sure I can get us a
seat, there are already quite a few people hanging out at the bar.
The place smells like stale beer and popcorn, but I'm lucky to
score a high top table over by the front window. The tables
aren't as sticky as I thought they would be, which has more to do
with the early hour than the cleanliness. Sitting on the high bar
stool facing the door, I take off my leather jacket and lay it on my
lap, since I don't trust placing it anywhere else. Almost
immediately, a server is in front of me.

"What can I getcha beautiful?" an auburn haired, blue-eyed guy in his 40's asks – his brogue slips through his smile, making the words come out like a song.

"I'll have whatever lager you have on draft, please," I reply, not returning his smile.

"You betcha," he replies jovially, and heads off to the bar with a spring in his step.

His cheery personality has me feeling guilty for my gloomy attitude. When the server comes back with my pint, I thank him with too much enthusiasm and flash him a giant smile. He looks completely taken aback, and has no idea what to do with my awkward response. My cheeks immediately turn bright pink and I quickly take a sip of my beer. Well, at least if I end up murdered and the police come around asking questions, he'll remember me.

Sitting and listening to the Irish music playing from some corner speakers and to the loud chatter from a group of guys at the bar, I sip my beer and wait.

A few minutes after 5 p.m. the door to the bar is quickly pushed open, and in rushes a disheveled, yet still attractive, Johnny Mesa. His eyes nervously dart around the room until they land on me, and he gives me a little wave. He stops at the bar to order something and strides over to take the seat across from me. He is wearing jeans, boots, and a wrinkled t-shirt. His hair doesn't know which way to go, and he hasn't shaved in a few days.

"It's nice to see you again, Verity," he says with that charm he just can't seem to turn off.

"It's nice to see you too, Johnny. I must say, you've looked better."

"Wow, my brother wasn't kidding, you don't pull a punch," Johnny says trying to laugh it off. "I definitely have felt better, that's for sure."

The server braves my weirdness to bring Johnny his beer. The poor guy avoids eye contact with me, not that I blame him. He must think I'm manic.

"Let me start by saying I'm really sorry for your loss. Chloe seemed like a bright, ambitious, sweet woman. This must be very hard for you." I watch him carefully, trying to gauge his response.

"Well, you know, Josh and I worked with her on a couple projects, but other than that, I didn't know her very well. But she seemed very sweet, and I feel awful for her family," he says looking down at his beer.

"Oh, you didn't know her very well?" I say, trying to hide my irritation. There's nothing I dislike more than being lied to. And this handsome guy across from me is really starting to piss me off.

"No, not really," he says, and looks up for a brief second. But he can't hold my gaze for more than a few seconds before he looks down again. He is one terrible liar. How the heck did he get away with cheating on his wife for so long? She must be totally clueless.

I reach into my bag that's on the table and pull out the photo I took from Chloe's room. I slide it across the table until it's right under his gaze. His whole body tenses up. He can't seem to move, not even his eyes. He continues to stare at the photo, his body rigid with emotion. And then he slowly looks up at me and meets my eyes. Big, fat tears are rolling down his cheeks.

"She insisted on taking this photo of us. I never would let her take any normally. This was the only photo we had. It was such a perfect moment. We were so happy, and she begged me to just take one photo. She swore she'd be careful and not show anyone. How could I say no?" He says with only a slight tremor in his voice. "Melissa, my wife, was away for work. We stayed in and cooked chicken and pasta, and drank wine. Chloe got to stay over for the first time, and that morning we had coffee in bed. The sun was shining through the windows and she looked so beautiful. I told her that, and that's when she begged me for the photo."

Two things are going through my mind as I listen to Johnny talk. First of all, although I don't want to, I can't help feeling bad for him. He clearly was in love with Chloe. But, I also keep thinking about his wife. The story of this photo tells me he had his mistress stay overnight and sleep in the bed he and his wife share. Total scumbag move. And, secondly, at this moment, sitting across from someone whom I suspect may have murdered a young woman - I have no fear. As I look into the eyes of this man, I know I am not looking at a murderer. I'm looking at a devastated man whose heart has been ripped out. He is wrecked. Lost.

"Does your wife know?"

"She does now. I just told her. I realized it was going to come out at some point. I thought as soon as they looked at Chloe's phone records they would see all the calls and texts between the two of us, and they would have been knocking down my door. I just couldn't keep the secret in any more. It was killing me."

We both stop and look at each other when he says that. Those words now carry more weight than either of us can hold.

I sip my beer. "I thought you killed her," I tell him flatly.

"What?! Are you crazy? I loved her. I was madly in love with her. I kept planning on telling Melissa, but of course it never seemed like a good time. There is never a good time to tell your wife you're not in love with her anymore! I'm an idiot. I will never forgive myself for that."

I realize the only thing Johnny is guilty of is infidelity. And it seems like he's being punished enough. Of course, he deserves it.

"Did you ever bring her to Jane Street? To the CFF building on Jane Street?"

"No, I didn't. I was only there that one time I met you."

"Can you think of any reason she would have been there? For work? With Josh, maybe?"

"No, Josh wouldn't have called her in yet. Josh would only use her when a project was finished, and she would stage it to get it ready to put on the market. So, he probably wouldn't have used her at your building. But he would have referred her to you, to use as an interior designer."

"That one time you were at Jane Street, I remember you and Josh arguing about something. Did he know about you and Chloe?"

"He had just recently figured it out. I'm not sure how. I think he saw us being too close at the latest apartment we worked on together in Tribeca.

"How did he take it?"

"Not well," Johnny says shaking his head. "He was fuming. He told me to break up with her or he wouldn't use me as his carpenter anymore. I don't think he was worried about Melissa, I think he was upset that it might ruin the business relationship with Chloe. He really liked working with her."

Before he can linger too much on the fact that they won't be working with Chloe anymore, I try and quickly change the topic.

"From what I gather, she trusted you more than anyone. Did she tell you what she was working on lately? Tina said she was really worried about something at work, but she wouldn't say what it was."

"She was an interior designer, not a spy. What could she have been working on that she wouldn't be able to talk about?" he says, clearly baffled.

"I don't know. But whatever it was, it got her killed."

Chapter 18

I cab home after meeting with Johnny. It's all just so depressing. I can't help but feel bad for that cheating bastard. Maybe it's because I know all too well what it's like to love and lose someone. I know how it feels to be completely alone - to traumatically have the way you view everything and everyone altered forever. Johnny's wife is leaving him and his mistress was murdered. Wait until the media gets ahold of this story. I don't think he realizes this is the calm before the storm. He hopefully has a good attorney.

The ring of my cell phone interrupts my gloomy thoughts. It's Evelyn, and since this is later than she'd normally call me, that's not a good sign.

"Hi, Evelyn. What's going on?"

"Verity, thank goodness I reached you." Evelyn sounds on the verge of hysterics.

"What's wrong?" I ask, afraid for the answer.

"I just found out through a friend at the *NY Post* who gave me a courtesy call. They are going to run a story tomorrow morning about David and the dead girl, I'm sorry, what's her name?"

"Chloe."

"Right, of course, Chloe. I'm sorry, I can't think."

"What about David and Chloe? He said she decorated the entire office. That's a big office. They must have 100 people working there that had interactions with her," I tell her calmly.

"Well, that's not the entire story," Evelyn says slowly.

"What do you mean? Did you know something?" I say, my voice getting louder.

Evelyn doesn't answer right away.

"Evelyn? What do you know that you didn't tell me?" I demand, trying to stay calm.

I hear Evelyn sigh. "David came over last night after the meeting," (was that only last night?), "and after a couple glasses of scotch, he started talking to Mitchell about the girl, Chloe."

I'm suddenly very tired.

"He said she wasn't decorating the entire office, she was only decorating three offices – David's being one of them. David and Chloe apparently stayed late one weeknight picking out some fabric for the furniture, and they ended up ordering food and he pulled out a bottle of wine. She took photos of their meal, and one photo of just the two of them, and she posted them on that instabook . . ."

"You mean Instagram," I say with no emotion. The cab is pulling up to my house and I pay the driver and get out. I'm so glad to be home.

"Yes, Instagram," Evelyn continues. "Well, of course the media found the photos online and the front page of tomorrow's paper will be the photo of David and Chloe smiling and clinking their glasses of wine together in a cheers."

How did I miss that photo on Chloe's Instagram page?

"Have you contacted Karen?"

"Who's Karen?" Evelyn asks.

"Karen McKenna. The PR woman from Specter Group," I say with as much patience as I can muster. "I'm assuming you haven't."

"Oh, no, I didn't do that. Should I do that?"

"I'll do it. But, I need to warn you, Evelyn. It sounds like it might be too late. This is not going to look good for us."

"I was afraid of that."

What I want to say to her is - this is a disaster. We have just found ourselves in the middle of a PR nightmare, and I don't know when we'll wake up.

Walking in my house, I collapse on the couch with my coat still on. It's only 7:15 but it feels like midnight. It has been a long day – between Tessa, Tina, Johnny and now this . . .what a mess. I need wine. As I pour myself a glass of wine, I wonder how I'm going to break the news to Karen. I guess the silver lining is, although there is no stopping the story at this point, at least we'll be prepared for it and can have a response ready.

Picking up my phone, I take a big sip of wine, and dial Karen's number – it's better to just get it over with.

"Hi, Karen," I say when she answers, "I'm about to ruin your night."

After about an hour on the phone with Karen, who handled the news like the professional she is, I feel like I could sleep for days. Karen is most likely going to be up most the night planning a response to tomorrow's bombshell news story. I have never been so thankful that we hired a PR Firm.

My mind won't turn off, so I know I'll never be able to fall asleep. I make myself one of my favorite meals, a platter of hummus, pita and veggies, and pour a second glass of wine. With the TV turned on to some old romantic comedy on HBO called *The Wedding Planner*, with Jennifer Lopez and Matthew McConaughey, I do my best to relax. I will never understand how people get so freaked out about a wedding. All that time and money – really? That will never be me. Well, maybe I'll spend some money on the dress. And the shoes.

Once I've had a chance to wind down, I'm so tired my whole body aches. Upstairs, I quickly get ready for bed and snuggle under the covers, and I'm asleep within minutes.

She's running through a field. The only sound is that of her labored breathing and the swishing of the knee-high grass as her legs cut through it. Risking being tripped by the tangled grass, she looks up and ahead - the house getting closer and closer. Once she finally reaches the brick house, she runs up the front steps two at a time. The number 76 is in gold letters on the door. Pushing through the door, she races to the back of the house. The kitchen. She knows he's not far behind her. She scans the mostly empty kitchen, looking for something. Darting from one end of the room to the next - panic begins to set in. She drops to the ground and scurries on her hands and knees, rubbing her hands across the floor all the way over to the cabinets. And then he's on her. The cold water startles her as her head is shoved under, her arms and legs flailing and fighting. Her eyes stare up at him until her world goes dark...

Chapter 19

He watches her get out of a cab in front of her multi-million dollar townhouse. She's all dressed up in her high heels and expensive coat. It must be nice to have money just given to you – to not have to work for it. She obviously didn't earn what she has, she works at a charity for god's sake.

The darkness is a natural cover as he skulks in the shadows of the streetlights. His big black coat and black wool hat offer extra invisibility. He pretends to be looking at his phone every now and then, just in case anyone notices him there, staring at her house. She walks up the front stairs to her castle, on the phone the whole time. He wishes he could just run across the street right now and strangle her. He can already feel his strong hands closing around her perfect neck. But that would be too risky. He's got to be smart about it. He's got to have it planned perfectly. He didn't think things through with Chloe and that led to a few mistakes that he still needs to clean up.

But it had to be done. Chloe was about to ruin all he had worked for. He didn't work tirelessly for years to have some stupid girl take it all away from him. What would his family think? He had to do it. It's what you have to do when you're at the top. Sacrifices have to be made. And sorry, Verity, but you're one of those sacrifices. You're asking too many questions and sticking your nose where it doesn't belong. Why do you care anyway? You didn't know Chloe. This is your fault, Verity, not mine. I've got to protect my livelihood.

I know just how to lure her in. She doesn't suspect me at all. She's always smiling at me and flirting with her eyes. This will be a piece of cake. The thought of her eyes reminds him of Chloe's eyes staring back at him as the life slowly left her body. His heart races as he remembers the fear and panic as she fought to stay alive. She knew he had all the power. He runs things. He makes the tough decisions. This thought boosts him up and he feels a high he never knew existed before that night. If he's going to be honest with himself, he's quite looking forward to that special moment with Verity. He can't wait to see that look of shock and fear as she realizes she's going to die, and he's the one deciding she doesn't get to live anymore.

All the money in the world can't save you now, Verity.

Chapter 20

If there's such a thing as sidewalk rage, I've got it. I want to push the people aside who are walking in front of me at a snail's pace and then decide to just stop dead in their tracks. Do they not realize this is rush hour in New York City? I wish there were separate sidewalks for locals and tourists. Yes, I'm in a bad mood. Waking up grumpy after that horrible nightmare - and I overslept. I didn't think I needed to set my alarm anymore. Now, I'm late. And with no time to exercise, my stress level is through the roof.

While at Roast for Evelyn's and my coffees, I was smacked in the face by an entire row of newspapers resting innocently below the front counter. The glaring front page of today's *Post* is that sickening photo of David and Chloe smiling as they clink their wine glasses together. The headline reads, in black bold letters:

SECRET AFFAIR LEADS TO MURDER?

By putting that question mark at the end of the headline these media outlets think they can get away with anything. David and his family must be so distraught.

I take a cab down to mid-town and the 44th Street block is closed down due to some type of utility work. The cab can't drop me in front of the CFF building, so now I'm walking behind these slow tourists, ready to scream. By the time I reach the CFF building, I'm practically sprinting. I guess that will suffice as today's workout.

Upon entering the CFF office, the lights are already on and I can hear Evelyn on the phone. I knock lightly on Evelyn's open office door so that I don't startle her. She waves me in with her hand as she continues talking on the phone. I put her coffee down on her desk in front of her, and plop down in one of the side chairs. After taking a long swig of my coffee, which tastes like water in the desert, I close my eyes, let out a big sigh and try to calm down.

When Evelyn hangs up the phone I ask her who she was speaking with.

"That was Charlie Petersen - he's concerned, to say the least. And he's not the first major donor to call me with questions about the girl, and about the CFF Home. 'Will the Home still be built? How long will construction be delayed?' It's going to be another long day."

"I guess you've seen this," I say to her as I pull a copy of the *Post* out of my purse.

"You bought one?!" Evelyn says in a shocked and accusatory tone.

"Well, we have to know what people are saying."

"I refuse to read that garbage. It's lies. All lies," Evelyn says angrily, as she smooth's the hair back from her face.

"I know it is, but I feel I have to read what it says anyway. Evelyn, don't worry, we'll figure this out. If David is innocent the police will not find any evidence to the contrary. He will be exonerated and, knowing him, he will most likely sue the *Post* for slander."

"What do you mean, *if* he's innocent?" Evelyn asks. "You can't possibly believe David could do something like this? He's been married for over 30 years to a wonderful woman. He has two children – two daughters! He would never do something like this."

"Of course he wouldn't," I say, and try to believe it.

It's not that I think David is guilty; I'm just not so quick to say someone's innocent. Having gone to law school, I saw what appeared to be ordinary people do some horrible things. And whenever that person's family and neighbors were interviewed, they would say, "I could never imagine so-and-so doing something like this. He seemed normal. He was a family man," and so on.

People are capable of anything if they feel they have no other option. Trust me when I say, there is always another option. It's just for some people that other option is too difficult to choose. If the other option can hurt them, hurt their family, lose them money, or all of the above, that's when they feel trapped. I'm looking at everyone through fresh eyes – David, Johnny, Josh . . . Ryker.

In my own office, I start to read the article on David. It is much more of a sensational piece than an article with real facts about David and Chloe. It's a headline grabber, and that's it. Although, one paragraph catches my eye:

David Cohen is a Partner at the Law Offices of Hancock, Metz and Cohen. Mr. Cohen is known for using shrewd tactics in the courtroom that skate on the edge of legality. Getting acquittals for high profile defendants, who were deemed 'Dead Men Walking' by prosecutors before a case, Mr. Cohen has been donned 'Cohen the Con' by many here in Manhattan. Mr. Cohen likes to win. Could this all have been about ego? Did poor Chloe Kingston refuse his advances? Or is this just karma coming back to bite the big con artist? Keep reading The Post *for more information on this case as it becomes available.*

Well, that's not good. I know Mitchell has been best friend's with David since grade school – could this blind Mitchell to the facts about him? I've never particularly warmed to the guy, but that's not too out of the ordinary for me. I don't warm to many people. Either way, if public opinion continues to view David negatively, I am going to have to have a conversation with Evelyn about asking David to step down from the Board. That is, if he's not already in jail.

Now feeling even grumpier, I put the David aside and get to the rest of my work. Listening to about one thousand voicemails from members of different media outlets asking me for a statement, reminds me to check the CFF website. Thankfully the statement Karen put together is on the front page of our site. It directs all media inquiries to Karen. I definitely don't envy her today. After deleting all the voicemails from the press on my work line, I start working my way through a million emails.

After a few hours of digging myself out of the email avalanche, I stand up to stretch out. I've been hunched over this computer without a break and I can feel it all over my body. I need another coffee. Or maybe some food. Grabbing my phone to see what time it is, I see that I somehow missed a text. It's from Ryker: *Still smiling from our dinner. Are you free tonight?*

Thinking of our dinner a few nights ago my insides get tingly and I start to blush.

I write back: *Possibly. What did you have in mind?*

I would like to play chef tonight. My place?

Those last two words stop me in my tracks, and I have to remind myself to breathe. Am I ready for his place? Are *we* ready for his place? I know what Tessa would tell me to do: "Go for it, Verity. Why don't you date anyone? Why do you push all men away? Blah, blah, blah."

Sure. I text back.

Please contain your enthusiasm ☺ *. See you at 8*

And just like that, my awful day has turned around. Or, so I thought.

It's hard for me to concentrate after the texts from Ryker. And since I've answered all my emails and voicemails, and my hands are tied working on anything regarding Jane Street, I decide to do some more research on Chloe.

What was she looking for in my dream last night? She was in the kitchen at Jane Street in the dream. Is she trying to tell me she was killed there? Maybe it's a metaphor – like she's looking for something at work – where I work. Perhaps it's in reference to what she was secretly researching – looking for. Wouldn't she have told Johnny if it had something to do with her job? Unless, maybe it was about Johnny? Or Josh? This would be a lot easier if she would just come out and tell me.

Pulling up Chloe's website on my computer again, I click on the "Happy Clients" tab. A slew of happy faces show up on my screen - men, women, couples, and families all with big smiles holding up some sort of piece of paper. I click on the first photo captioned "Margaret Wilson, Park Slope." The photo is that of an African American woman, I would guess in her mid-50's, holding up a piece of paper. There are also before and after photos of her home.

Zooming in on the photo of the woman, I see that the paper she's holding says "Certificate of Completion." After a little research on a Certificate of Completion I learn:

A final inspection is required when all work has been completed. When it has been determined that the project meets the applicable codes and standards, a Certificate of Completion or a Certificate of Occupancy will be issued.

After a quick Internet search I find Margaret Wilson's LinkedIn page. It looks like she works in finance. I'm not even sure what I'm going to say to her, or why I'm calling, but once I see a phone number, I start to dial. On the third ring a friendly voice answers, "Hello, Margaret here."

"Hi Margaret. My name is Verity Townsend."

"Hello Verity, what can I help you with?"

"I was a friend of Chloe Kingston. She helped you design your home?"

Complete silence.

"Hello? Margaret?" I ask, wondering if the call got dropped.

"Yes, sorry. I'm still here. I'm just trying to get used to her name being used in the past tense."

"I know. I understand. I was hoping you could tell me a little bit about when you two worked together."

"Sure. I already told the detective everything, not that there's much to tell."

Score one for Detective O'Donnell - he beat me to it.

"So did Chloe do interior design work for you?"

"Yes, interior design and so much more. She was just starting out and was anxious to get some clients. She did the whole renovation design and then once the construction work was finished, she did the interior design, picking the paint colors, furniture, and textiles – all that stuff. She was excited to have the work, and didn't charge me much at all. She was really very talented. We had a lot of fun together."

"I see. So did Chloe hire the contractor?"

"Yes, she did."

"Was it Josh Mesa?" I ask her.

"Um, no. The contractor's name was Charlie something-or-other. But why does that Mesa name sound familiar?"

My heart sinks. I don't know why I even think that would be important. I suppose I was hoping for some sort of connection.

"Oh, okay. Thank you, Margaret. I really appreciate you taking the time to speak with me," I say, trying to hide my disappointment.

When I get off the phone with Margaret, I feel defeated. I'm not sure what to do next. I'm not a detective. Staring out my window down at the busy world below on 44th Street, I watch people stop at the small fruit stand on the corner. People everywhere rushing around while they talk on their phones. My mind keeps going over and over everything I've learned so far, and honestly, it's not much. But Tina said Chloe was worried about something at work. This has to be about that – it just has to be. I have to start with her clients. Although it seems overwhelming, I know what I have to do. I have to call every single one of the people on her website and see what I can find. It'll be just like law school – all the tedious research. But, just like my favorite teacher, Professor Blake, always said – "dig deeper." He said cases are won by whichever team dug the deepest. He also said, "If you can't dazzle them with your brilliance, baffle them with your bullshit." He was the best.

I begin to search the Internet for all the different names on Chloe's website client list. Hours go by as I stare at my computer, searching. My desk is covered in post-it notes and lists. This really is like law school. Halfway through the list I head downstairs to the little lunch place on the street level of our building. I stretch a little and let my eyes adjust to the real world. I order a salad to go and plant myself back at my desk, and dig deeper.

Once I have the contact information for all the people listed under the "Happy Clients" tab on Chloe's site, I start making phone calls. Most people want to talk to me about how sweet Chloe was, and how they can't believe she's gone. "Who would do such a thing?" was asked too many times to count. I take solid notes on all the clients and where they live, and what services Chloe provided. I print out the photos of each person holding their Certificate of Completion, to match them to my notes. Thorough doesn't even begin to explain my process. Sometime during the mayhem, Evelyn knocks and tells me she's heading home. I don't even know what time it is, but it feels good to do something, even if it may not lead to anything. False progress, perhaps.

When I hang up with the last client on the list, I sit back with a sigh. Photos, papers, post-it notes, and highlighters clutter my desk. And after all that work, what am I left with? Nothing. Nada. Zilch.

No issues, no angry clients, and not one of them even used Josh Mesa as the contractor. I guess Chloe only started working with Josh recently? Or maybe she just staged apartments for him, but she never recommended him to her clients to be their contractor? Well, that says something . . .

Or, maybe she did use him and it didn't work out well, and those people aren't listed on her "Happy Clients" tab. There are still just too many unknowns. Perhaps I should meet with Josh. But will he tell me the truth if one of his client's wasn't happy? He still desperately wants to impress me, and Ryker of course. Ryker.

Oh no, what time is it? I look at my phone and see that it's 7:38. I have to go! This will all have to wait until tomorrow. I turn off my computer and attempt to straighten out my desk, but then quickly give up. I check myself in the office bathroom mirror and am a little horrified. My hair is sticking out all over, I have dark circles under my eyes, and I'm even more pale than normal. I quickly brush my hair and then, with wet hands, try and smooth down the fly-aways at the part. I dab some concealer under my eyes to hide the dark circles, and add a little blush to my pale cheeks. Lastly, I swipe on my signature red lipstick. That'll have to do.

On the elevator ride down to the street level of the building, I pull up the Uber app on my phone – and reserve a car that is 7 minutes away. Outside on the noisy street, I can feel the energy from the people as they are freed from work for the day. As if by the miracle of darkness, the city's people become cheerful with a renewed sense of possibilities. New York has a cranky morning commute, but the city definitely comes alive at night. The energy is infectious and I join my fellow New Yorkers in putting the long day behind me, and getting excited for what lays ahead.

Lost in the New York moment, I don't immediately see the man approaching me until he is so close that I feel something brush against my arm. I turn to my left and see a man slightly taller than me wearing a black wool hat, and a hooded sweatshirt with the hood up over his head. His face is turned away from me. He seems to be looking at something to his left, so I follow his gaze. A tall man, with skin the color of deep mahogany, in a long black wool coat and black leather gloves is walking toward me and the mystery man. As the tall man gets closer I realize I recognize him from somewhere. Before I can make the connection, the man smiles a broad smile showing large white teeth. How do I know him? The man's eyes shift toward the hat wearing man next to me and his smile fades. I turn my head further around to see who it is standing next to me – but he's gone. Poof. The guy disappeared.

The tall man reaches me and says in an accent that reminds me of my most recent island vacation, "Hello Ms.

Townsend, I am Kymani. We have met on a few occasions. I work for Mr. Rensselaer, and I would be honored to drive you to your dinner at his home this evening."

He sent his driver. Nice move, Mr. Rensselaer.

Chapter 21

Of course. Of course, Ryker lives in the Merkin House building. Even being relatively new to New York City, I know the Merkin House building and its reputation as one of the most sought after buildings, not just in Tribeca, but all of Manhattan. It's only seven floors high, but the location and the extravagance of the apartments are legendary. Manhattan's elite bribe and blackmail to get into this building. I wonder which method Ryker used.

"It's the Penthouse, Ms. Townsend," Kymani tells me as he opens the front door to the building for me. He then uses a key in the elevator to access the seventh floor. As the elevator climbs the seven flights I can't help but feel a flutter low in my belly. As the elevator doors slide open, I am immediately greeted by Ryker's smiling face, in a gallery style entry hall - my heart all but stops. Why does he have to be so good looking?

He's dressed casually in a pair of dark denim jeans tailored to fit his long, lean body perfectly. He has on a blue striped button down shirt, untucked, with the sleeves rolled up his forearms neatly, and leather shoes the color of smooth cognac. His dark hair, which is normally combed back sleekly, is falling forward over his brow, as if he got out of the shower, dried it with a towel and let it be – deliberately disheveled. His easy smile can't hide the intensity behind his deep-set blue eyes. The small flutter in my lower belly is now a strong flapping beat moving up from my belly to my heart. The thronging is so pronounced I fear Ryker might be able to hear it, so I quickly say something to cover the sound.

"Hello, Mr. Rensselaer."

"Good evening, Ms. Townsend. Please come in," he says as he steps aside to allow me further into the loft. I was so preoccupied looking at Ryker, I hadn't noticed the apartment behind him - if you could even call it an apartment. It is really more like an estate sitting on the top floor of a building. If I could control my jaw from dropping when I got the first glimpse of Ryker, I'm not sure I can control it now. As I walk into the great room I am completely taken aback. The entire back stretch of wall is floor to ceiling windows, as is half of the ceiling. Hanging from the glass 20 foot ceiling is an enormous light fixture, which is more like an art installation - about 50 glass globes hang at different lengths all lit up like stars in the sky. It's truly breathtaking. Two doublewide sliding glass doors along the back wall open up to reveal an enormous patio with a stone gas fireplace, two L-shaped couches, a full outdoor kitchen and dining table. The east-facing views of the city are spectacular.

In the living room, there are floating steps leading up to a loft on the second floor, and behind the steps I see a temperature controlled wine room with a glass door displaying the wine like art.

So caught up in the perfection that is his apartment, I haven't said a word since I arrived. Stopping to look at Ryker, who is leaning against a light gray couch just watching me, all I can say is, "Wow."

"Thank you?" He laughs. "I can see you have excellent taste."

"When did you buy this place?" I ask him, unable to hide my curiosity.

"About a year ago now. One of the perks of working in real estate is that I get first dibs. I heard a rumor that the previous owner was thinking of selling and I jumped on it before it could hit the market."

"Wow," I say again. "I have never seen anything like it," I say continuing to look around.

"I'll show you around some more later. First, can I offer you a drink?"

"I would love one, thank you. A glass of wine would be great."

"Of course, how about a Pinot Noir?" Ryker asks.

"That sounds perfect," I tell him.

Ryker walks over to a marble wet bar and opens a bottle of wine. He pours two generous size glasses of wine and offers me one.

"That's quite a heavy pour you have," I tease him. "I hope you're not trying to get me drunk."

"I wouldn't think of such a thing," Ryker says with a devilish grin. "Let's sit outside in front of the fire. It's a beautiful night."

I follow Ryker outside onto the patio and the view of the city strikes me again. It's a magical feeling being surrounded by all the lights from the buildings, as the buzz of the city drones on below like background music.

We sit on a couch next to a slate gas fireplace. I notice there are a few plates of cheeses, crackers, and fruit already on the outdoor coffee table. Ryker lets me sit directly next to the fireplace, which is the warmest spot, and he sits down next to me. I turn to face him and hold up my glass of wine in a toast.

"To a beautiful night, with the most beautiful woman," Ryker says as he clinks his wine glass with mine.

Normally I would find a line like that completely cheesy, and would probably roll my eyes. But somehow, in this setting, with this guy, it just seems sweet. I look down shyly and am thankful for the cover of night, so he can't see me blush.

After a few sips of wine, we fall into a relaxed conversation. I ask him about his family and where he grew up. As he talks I realize I don't know a lot about him. He was born and raised in Manhattan, the youngest of three, with two older sisters. My assumption that Ryker came from money is confirmed as he describes his workaholic father, who made a fortune on Wall Street, and his mom who had her own clothing line. Her line was sold in boutiques all around the country. His parents got divorced when he was 8 years old, and he split his time between their two apartments, which were only a block away from each other on the Upper East Side. He tells funny stories about how when he was in high school he would get away with being out at clubs in the city by telling each of his parents he was at the other's house. They hated each other so much they would never have called each other to check up on the story - so Ryker got away with a lot. He laughs about the wild times he had in his teens. I smile, enjoying all his stories, and picturing a young Ryker wreaking havoc on New York City.

"With that being said, I think I got a lot of the wild years out of my system early. Once I graduated from Columbia I was completely ready to get serious. A lot of people assume I was given everything I have, but my father believed in making your own way. I started out with nothing. I was a little bitter about it at first, to be honest. I felt like my grandfather gave my father a head start, and part of me felt I was owed something. But I soon realized how wrong I was. The biggest gift my father could have given me was the feeling of succeeding on my own. Doing it by myself, for myself. It lit a fire under me, and I hustled knowing I wouldn't eat that week if I didn't turn a commission," with this Ryker smiles.

"I knew I wanted to work in real estate, so I started working for a real estate development firm right after graduation. I was doing all aspects of real estate back then – I would even do the renovation work myself in order to save money. You should see me work a table saw," Ryker says with a laugh.

"Ryker Rensselaer doing manual labor? I'd have to see it to believe it," I say with a laugh.

"Oh, believe it. But, it wasn't long before I realized I had a knack for real estate development, got lucky on a few big deals, and started my company a few years later. And, here we are now," he says. Although Ryker is downplaying his success, I know better. I know for someone as young as he is, and to do what he has done with real estate in this city, he must have worked relentlessly.

"Well, I feel like I've been monopolizing the conversation here. And although I typically like to monopolize, well, everything," he smiles, "I have to admit I am dying to find out more about the mysterious Verity. But first, I'm starving. Let's go inside and have dinner."

Inside, Ryker walks over to the bar and refills both our wine glasses. "Come with me into the kitchen, we can chat while I prepare the food."

"Wait, are you telling me that *you* are going to make dinner?" I say, shocked.

"Don't look so surprised, Ms. Townsend. I know my way around a kitchen. Well, okay, some of this I had Maria make ahead of time," Ryker says and we both laugh.

"Who's Maria?" I ask.

"Oh, so you're the jealous type," Ryker teases me. I roll my eyes, and make sure he sees me do it. "Maria is like my surrogate mom. She cleans, she cooks, she takes my clothes to the dry cleaners . . . I don't know what I'd do without her."

I follow Ryker into the custom kitchen, done in grays, white and gold. The floors are a light gray wood laid in a chevron pattern. The walls are white, with custom millwork everywhere, the countertops are marble, and there are two refrigerators, a Viking 8 burner stove and double ovens. Gorgeous gold pendant lights hang over the island. I pull up a stool at the large marble-topped island, ready to watch Ryker in action. Or, well, heat up some already prepared food.

"Okay, so now, tell me something about you that I don't know, Verity."

"There's not much to tell. I grew up in Albany, went to law school, realized I didn't want to be a lawyer, and then took the job with CFF and moved to New York. Not very exciting."

"Oh come on. You gotta do better than that," Ryker says as he pulls a salad out of the refrigerator, and dresses it. "Do you have any siblings?" He asks.

"No siblings. I'm an only child."

"Wow, you're really going to make this difficult aren't you?" Ryker says.

"Make what difficult?"

"Letting me get to know you," Ryker says, as he stops what he's doing and looks directly into my eyes.

"What about your parents? Are they still in Albany funding your fabulous New York City lifestyle?"

I know Ryker grew up wealthy, and all of his friends most likely grew up wealthy. In his circle, parents' funding a child's lavish lifestyle is common. For this reason, I will not take his comment personally, and will resist the urge to verbally attack him.

"No. My parents died when I was young. My Aunt Marion raised me. She also passed away right before I moved to New York."

Ryker stops slicing the French bread, and looks at me.

"I'm so sorry, Verity. That must have been very difficult. Now I understand your passion for CFF. And your independence."

I take a sip of my wine.

"It was a long time ago. But yes, that is why CFF means so much to me. I know what it's like to not have family. Helping these kids find a place to call home, and families to surround them has just been so unbelievably rewarding. I'm lucky to be able to work where my passion lies, without any concern for the size of my paycheck. I understand how ridiculously fortunate that makes me."

Ryker nods his head. He's putting some salmon on a baking sheet and then puts the sheet in the oven. "You are fortunate to not have to worry about money, however, this is only due to the loss of your family. And you work for a charity, when you don't *need* to be working at all. No guilt necessary on your part," Ryker says matter-of-factly. I stop drinking my wine mid-sip, stunned that he would pick up on the guilt I often feel being a 28-year-old who will never need to worry about money.

"I'm a bit embarrassed to be telling you this after hearing how you earned what you have the hard way. But my parents left me money," I say looking down at my wine, these are not things I normally tell people."And I didn't know about it or receive it until I was 21, so I actually grew up very modestly."

"And now look at you, taking Manhattan by storm in your Prada dress and Jimmy Choo's. You must be a quick study," Ryker says, lightening the mood. I can't help but chuckle.

"I have enjoyed the shopping." This has both of us laughing.

We sit at the vast dining table, with the amazing light fixture twinkling above us. The doors to the patio are open and the view is hard to look away from. The meal consists of salmon, salad, wild rice and fresh crusty bread, which I even allow myself to enjoy. It must be the wine. As we eat, the conversation somehow leads to Chloe, and I feel like I'm being dragged back to reality.

"How about that headline in the *Post*?" Ryker says. "Man, if that wasn't a punch in the gut, right?"

"It was seriously awful. Poor David. I mean, so the two of them got some take-out working late one night. Why does the media always have to make the story into something ugly?"

"Well, there might be more to that story . . ." Ryker says slowly.

"What do you mean?"

Ryker looks uncomfortable, but now that he started it, he knows I'm not going to let it go.

"Let's just say David has been known to come on a little strong to, you know, *young* ladies."

"David? No way. I don't believe it. He has a family! A sweet wife, two grown daughters . . . How do you know this?" I'm all worked up now.

"I'm sorry I brought it up," Ryker says. "Can I blame the wine?"

"Seriously, Ryker, you have to tell me. Who told you this about David? Maybe it's just a horrible rumor."

"Well, he's sort of a regular at Ice. I always hook him up and let him sit in the VIP area, of course. And some of the female servers have told me stories. He hits on lots of the servers, and lots of other women at the club – and let's just say they all have a certain age in common. Young. I mean, I'm only 36 so when I say someone's young, they're *really* young."

Talk about a punch in the gut. I feel so naïve and betrayed. My jaw is hanging open, and I can't seem to find any words.

"I'm so sorry I told you this. This is the last thing you need to be worrying about right now. I know what you need – you need chocolate! Let's have some dessert. Maria made her famous chocolate molten cake, it's unbelievable," Ryker says, trying really hard to change the subject.

"I'm just stunned," I admit. "I really thought I knew him. And it also hurts my ego a bit – I consider myself to be a pretty good judge of character. I wouldn't have seen this coming from a mile away."

"I guess there's not much that surprises me anymore. I've seen people do some pretty messed up things," Ryker says. "Growing up here, and then dealing with the monsters in real estate development in New York . . . The length some people will go to in order to make a deal, or save some money -- it's pretty crazy," he says shaking his head.

David at Ice? Gross. "Wait, did you know that Chloe had been to Ice?"

"I didn't know that, no. Although I try and make an appearance there on the weekend nights, I certainly don't know everyone who's there," Ryker says. Does he sound extra defensive?

"How do you know she was at Ice?" Ryker asks.

"I saw photos on her Instagram page of her there," I tell him.

"You're studying her Instagram page, Verity? I hope you're not doing anything too risky, or, for lack of a better term, stupid. Just let the police handle it."

"Could she have been there with David?!" I gasp, ignoring Ryker's warning.

"I have no idea. But like I was saying, people are shady. We don't even know anything about Chloe. I certainly didn't know her well. I've seen people do worse things to get ahead. That's why I know when I see something good," he says, looking right into my eyes. He moves his hand to cover my hand on the table, and I can feel the warmth emanating from his skin.

Ryker stands up, still holding my hand, and gently tugs me up to standing. Our bodies are inches from each other, as he puts his other hand on my lower back, slowly pulling me closer. It's as if time has stopped, as I get lost in his intense deep blue eyes. I put my other hand lightly on his back and he leans down and kisses me softly. I can feel the passion behind it. I close my eyes and take in his musky, sweet smell. I know how much more he wants, and I want it too. We're both flushed and almost panting with desire. But, I'm not quite ready.

I pull back, and break the spell. I take a deep breath and smile at him. He smiles back at me, understanding I'm stopping things now, because if we go even a little further, there's no turning back.

"I'm going to use the bathroom, can you point me in the right direction?" I ask him.

"Of course," Ryker says, his voice sounds hoarse, "why don't you use the one at the top of the stairs," he points behind me to the floating steps. "First door on your right. I'll get the dessert and coffee ready."

I walk up the stairs, feeling a little shaky and anxious, and . . . excited. I have really enjoyed getting to know Ryker better. Turning down the hallway, I see the bathroom door and, almost immediately, I know something's wrong. I push open the door and that horrible sweet smell surrounds me. I feel like I can't breathe, and my knees give out. I look, and on the beautiful stone sink top, there's a candle burning. Panic sets in and I'm now gasping for breath. I crawl out of the bathroom on my hands and knees and back into the hallway. My head is spinning with what this could mean. I somehow make it down the steps, grasping the banister for dear life. Shaking.

Ryker comes around the corner from the kitchen, about to say something to me, but then he sees me, and his face turns to worry. "Verity. What is it? What's wrong? Are you okay?" He walks quickly over to me, and goes to wrap his arm around my waist to help me stand. I push his arm away, shaking my head, trying to find the words. I can't have him touching me. I just keep shaking my head, as I do my best to make it to the front door as quickly as I can. Ryker is right behind me, continuing to say my name and ask me what happened, what's wrong.

"The candle," I whisper as the elevator door closes.

Chapter 22

I wake up the next morning in bed, sweaty and miserable. Sleep came only after hours of tossing and turning. Thinking about my dream night that turned into a nightmare, I can't shake the look on Ryker's face as the elevator door closed. When I mentioned the candle, the confusion on his face turned to something else, was it understanding? Does he know what that candle signifies? How well did he know Chloe? I roll over onto my back as my mind continues the endless spin of uncertainty. Today – I'm not going into work. I am going to do some serious research on Chloe, candles, Ryker, David – anyone associated with Chloe and her job.

And Chloe – where has she been? Why has she stopped haunting my dreams, leaving me clues, opening and slamming doors? I need help for crying out loud! Ugh. I also need coffee.

Reluctantly getting out of bed, I go downstairs for a caffeine fix. I sit with my coffee in my oversized side chair and stare out the window. Outside the weather seems to match my mood - gray clouds fill the sky, and it looks cold and dreary. Wind kicks leaves around the streets and people hustle by with their heads down, bundled up, clutching their jackets to their bodies.

After I finish one cup of coffee, I pour another and dare to look at my phone. I see four missed calls from Ryker, and 2 text messages. I look at the texts first: *Verity, what happened? Please call me.* And: *I'm worried. Please please call me.*

I can't deal with that right now.

I turn on my laptop and send an email to Evelyn, telling her I'm not feeling so great, and that I need a day at home. And then, because it's me, I make a list of things I need to follow up on and research. In order to stay sane, I'm going to pretend I'm back in law school, and approach this like a case.

First, what do I know already: Chloe was murdered, I believe drowned, and buried at Jane Street. She was secretly dating a married man, and researching something at work that she didn't want anyone to know about. She worked for both David and Ryker. David most likely hit on her. How did she react? Did Ryker hit on her too? Nope, don't go there. Supposed to be sticking to the facts here. Chloe had a laptop that is missing. After contacting all her "Happy Clients," nothing suspicious arose. Is it strange that none of her "Happy Clients" used Josh Mesa? Or, to put it another way, that none of Josh Mesa's clients ended up on her "Happy Clients" list?

Well, I know they worked together on that Tribeca apartment. I can find out the name of the people that bought it and call them. I can find their name, the name of the candle that was burning in Ryker's bathroom, and perhaps call David and Josh? I'll start with the candle. I think I would recognize the candle label if I saw it again. It was a cream color, and I think the first word in the label was Jo.

I do an Internet search for images of "Jo candle." I know the label when I see it – Jo Malone, must be a popular brand of candles, although I've never heard of it. I scroll through all the Jo Malone candle photos and I see it. I click on the photo of the Jo Malone, Peonies and Blush Suede candle. I read the description:

"Peonies in voluptuous bloom. Flirtatious with the juicy bite of red apple and the opulence of jasmine, rose and gillyflower." The pungent floral smell, with fruit and jasmine.

I know that's the smell. I have no idea what gillyflower is, but I know this is it. It's at a department store for $450. Seriously? Rich people are crazy.

I'm feeling encouraged having found the candle with the smell that has been haunting me for the past week. The downside, however, is that the candle is very common. You can buy these candles everywhere. Does this mean Chloe was killed somewhere with this candle burning as she died? The thought makes me shiver. Especially since, right now, the only person I know who owns this candle is Ryker.

The next order of business – to find out who lives in that Tribeca apartment that Josh Mesa just remodeled and sold. I know Chloe decorated when Josh was finished with the renovation. I find the address from my texts with Josh, and search for the name of the person who purchased it. Maybe the sale was too recent, because nothing is popping up on the Internet. I could always ask Josh or Johnny for the new buyer's name - but then I'd have a lot of explaining to do. And I am not in the mood to explain.

Wait, I know where the apartment is- - I can just knock on their door and pretend I'm someone looking to use Josh as a contractor. I can ask them questions about their experience with him. But first, there's one more person I need to do some research on. I do another Internet search. This time I type in "David Cohen, esq., New York" and about a million articles pop up. How is it that I never thought to do a search on him? I guess, since he was already in place on the Board long before I started working at CFF, and since he has been a friend of Mitchell's for so long, I just took him at face value. I will never make that mistake again.

After reading many articles about cases David has worked on, I realize I don't really know what I'm looking for. I think I need to talk to people that deal with him everyday, people that see him for who he truly is – the good, the bad and the ugly. I need to go back down to Hancock, Metz and Cohen and talk to some co-workers. And then I will go down to the Tribeca Park building and speak with the new owners of Apartment 6C.

With my new plan set out before me, I'm re-energized. I quickly get dressed in black denim, a cream lace top and taupe ankle boots. A black wool coat that hits mid-thigh and has a big warm fur hood finishes off my outfit. With my hair down and straight, I put on minimal makeup – just mascara and lipstick, and I'm ready.

The last time I was at Hancock, Metz and Cohen was last Friday for the purchase of Jane Street. It was such a happy day – it seems like a million years ago. Walking into the beautifully appointed law office, I'm now wishing I were wearing something a little more professional. I clearly am not thinking straight today. Jeans - really? Oh well. I walk up to the receptionist, Monica, whom I have met and spoken to many times.

"Hi Monica, how are you?" I ask her politely, offering her a big smile.

"Verity! It's nice to see you. Did you have an appointment with Mr. Cohen today? Oh no, I didn't see it on the calendar. He's actually not here right now," Monica says nervously rambling.

"Oh, no, I didn't have an appointment. I was just going to pop in and see how Mr. Cohen is doing. Do you have any idea what time he'll be back?"

"I don't, but you can go ask Francine. You know Francine, right? David's personal Executive Assistant?"

"Yes, of course I know Francine. Thanks, Monica."

With everything playing out in the media the way it is, it seems everyone here at Hancock, Metz and Cohen is pretty on edge. It's clear Monica seems shaky and not herself. A small part of me begins to feel bad for David, but then I remember what Ryker told me about Ice, and that sympathy quickly disappears.

I walk through the long hallway to the back offices where David's assistant, Francine, sits. As I get closer I see the stress on Francine's face. She's talking on the phone with someone who clearly is not happy. As Francine sees me approach her desk, she offers me a weak smile and a little wave, but there's no joy to be found on her face. Obviously, she is having a rough day. This might not bode well for me.

I wait patiently a few steps away from Francine's desk giving her time to finish up her conversation. Francine is in her mid-50's and wearing a matching cornflower blue shell and cardigan sweater set. Her unnaturally red hair is cut into a short, layered look with wavy bangs. As she talks to this unknown caller, she must say "I'm so sorry" and "I apologize" a dozen times. That can't be good. When she finally is able to end the call and hang up the phone, she looks up at me and lets out a giant sigh.

"Hi, Verity, honey. How are you?" Francine says, trying her best to sound like her usual cheerful self.

"I think the better question is, how are *you*?"

"Oh, I'm surviving. I'm guessing you saw the article in the *Post* yesterday?"

I just nod my head.

"Well, that has caused quite a tizzy around here. The phone has been ringing off the hook with some of the clients David is currently defending. Many are afraid this will hurt their cases, which it won't, of course. At least I don't think so. Oh, and forget about Bill and Allen," Francine says referring to Bill Hancock and Allen Metz, the other two partners at the firm. "Bill and Allen are out of their minds with worry. They really read David the riot act this morning. But you don't want to hear about all of this, I'm sorry to bore you with office politics. What can I do for you? You know David's not here right now, right?"

"Yes, Monica told me David isn't here right now. Do you know when you expect him back?"

"Honestly, I don't. Please don't tell him I'm telling you this, but I don't even know where he went. After his meeting with Bill and Allen, he stormed out of the office and didn't tell anyone where he was going. Not even me. In 15 years as his assistant, I have never seen him so angry," Francine tells me in a loud whisper.

I knew I could count on Francine for the good gossip.

"Okay, no problem. Maybe you can help me. As I said, I did read that article in the *Post* yesterday and I was surprised by the way they described David. 'Cohen the Con' - is this really how he is viewed in the law world?"

Francine looks a little uncomfortable.

"Look, this is just the two of us, Francine. You know David and Mitchell Campbell are childhood friends. I just want to know all the information so I can make informed statements to the media if I need to." I'm trying my best to gain her confidence and let her know we're on the same side.

Francine rubs her bright pink lipsticked lips together. "David is very good at his job. He has won many high profile cases where his client was thought to have no chance of acquittal. I think this can cause a lot of jealousy within his profession. And obviously, this makes most prosecutors frustrated with him.

"Has there ever been an official complaint filed against him for the tactics he uses in the courtroom?"

"There has never been an official complaint. Unofficially, there have been a lot of complaints about him. But David stays within the law. That's his job."

And now, I have to ask the tough question.

"Francine, and please be honest here, has there ever been any problems in the office with David? I don't know how to put this . . . Has David ever hit on any of the women in the office?" And now we're both uncomfortable.

"Verity, I'm not sure what rumors you're hearing, but on the record here, all I can say is that David has always treated me with respect. He has been nothing but professional and polite to me."

I nod my head and look down at my hands, feeling a little guilty for putting Francine in this position. It's her boss I'm asking her about, and she doesn't want him to look bad.

"Off the record," Francine starts to say, and my head pops up to look at her. We look each other in the eyes, and Francine motions for me to come closer. I lean in close enough to where I can smell her strong floral perfume.

Francine continues in a whisper, "Off the record, and I will deny ever saying this if asked again, David does have a wandering eye. He also can be a bit touchy-feely, for lack of better of term. He has never done anything inappropriate to me, but I'm a little too mature for his taste, if you understand what I'm saying."

"I think I completely understand." So it's true - David is a shady flirt. Why do people always have to be so disappointing?

"Thank you so much for your honesty, Francine. I just have one last question before I go. Did you ever meet Chloe Kingston?"

"I did meet that poor girl," Francine says, getting upset. "She was here quite a bit while helping with the interior design. She was sweet as pie. I can't believe something so awful happened to her. Who would want to kill an innocent thing like Chloe?"

With that last question hanging in the air, Francine and I just stare at each other. Once Francine understands what I'm silently asking, her eyes bug out and her mouth drops open.

"Now Verity, you know David. He may have his faults, and no one's denying that, but there is no way he would be capable of doing something like this. You know that!" Francine says in a shocked tone.

"I know, I know. I'm so sorry. This whole situation has me turned inside out. Of course I know David could never do something like that. But ... did you ever see him hit on her?" I ask quietly.

I feel like I'm working Francine's last nerve right now, but she's too polite to say anything.

"I never saw any behavior like that. But, she was definitely his type ..."

In a daze, I leave Hancock, Metz and Cohen. I'm trying to attach the previous version of who David Cohen is with the new version just described to me, and they seem like two different people. Is this why David dragged out the permit process?

A few blocks from the attorney's office the smell of a street vendor's hot dogs disrupts my perplexed thoughts. It's probably around 3 p.m. and I haven't eaten since breakfast. I see a salad spot up ahead and take a minute to sit at the window bar and enjoy a chopped salad with chicken in a vinaigrette dressing. My mind can't help but go over all the interactions I had with David leading up to this week. How did I miss the signs? With me, he has always been professional and reliable – not warm and cozy, but that wouldn't be how people describe me either.

And then my mind wanders to Ryker. Was I unfair to leave him like that? Does he think I'm a complete lunatic? I just saw that candle and panicked. I know he worked with Chloe in some capacity, and since this smell has infiltrated my nightmares, I just associate it with death and murder. To smell it in Ryker's bathroom ... just thinking about it now gives me the chills. That candle is a sign from Chloe. I'm just not sure what it means.

Finished with my salad, I head back out onto the streets of the city. As I pass by a funky café called Jacked Up Coffee, the promise of a caffeine jolt lures me in. The café has an eclectic vibe with mismatched tables and chairs, bright white walls are filled with modern art created by local artists, and the clientele is young and hip. Free Wi-Fi is of course available, so men and women staring at their laptops and tablets occupy most of the tables. I walk up to the fire engine red counter (that'll wake you up!), and order an Americano. As I wait for my coffee, I glance to my left toward the back wall of the café, and I can't believe my eyes. Standing out like a sore thumb in this youthful spot, sits David Cohen – and he's not alone. He sits across from a girl with dark, long wavy hair who appears to be very upset. A tissue is balled up in one hand, and her eyes are puffy. David looks upset in a different way – he looks angry. With a body so tense it could snap, he strains to keep his voice down. Using enough control to not bang, his fisted hands tap the table as he talks.

The young barista has to say my name four times before I hear her. Seeing David has me feeling a little panicky, which is odd. I'm not sure what to do - my initial thought is to grab my coffee and run out of there. But I pause, wondering if I should go confront him. Instead, I slink toward the back of the café and slip into one of only three booths against the sidewall. It's not the closest booth to where David and the mystery woman are sitting, but it's as close as I can get without being noticed. I slide down in the black leather booth with my back to David, and pretend to look at my phone. I try to drown out the surrounding chatter and focus on David's voice.

"What do you want from me, Dee? I'm doing the best I can."

"I just want you to tell me where you were - and I want you to be honest."

"I've told you a hundred times -- I was working. Whether you believe me or not is up to you. There's nothing I can do about that."

"Well, I don't believe you. Why should I? All you've ever done is lie to me – why should you start telling the truth now?" The girl's voice is shaking, and I'm pretty sure she's crying again.

There are a few muffled words, and then I hear a loud bang on the table. Slinking lower in my booth, with my head turned down at my phone, I shift my eyes to the left just as David whooshes past me in a huff. I watch him stomp out, knowing if he could have slammed the café door, he would have – like a toddler having a tantrum. Is that what happens when David doesn't get his way? He glances back over his shoulder with venom in his eyes, looking toward the back of the café toward Dee -- did he just see me? And then he's gone.

As far as I can tell, "Dee" hasn't moved. I'm uncharacteristically nervous to confront her, but I know this might be my only chance to find out who she is, and what type of relationship she has with David. Slowly, I slide out of the booth and nonchalantly walk to the back of the café. "Excuse me," I interrupt her phone-staring, "Do you know where I can find the ladies room?"

The red eyes staring back at me belong to an attractive woman in her mid-30s. A quick glance at her ring finger and I see she's not married. She's wearing a fitted charcoal grey suit with a cream shell underneath. A little boring; generic. My guess would be an entry to mid-level office job. Acting surprised to see her tears, I say, "Let me guess – guy trouble."

Looking slightly embarrassed, Dee casts her eyes down and away from me and laughs a little, and says "Is it that obvious?"

"Red, puffy eyes. Tears. Balled up tissue – young pretty woman sitting alone. Classic case of asshole boyfriend."

Dee looks startled with the mention of the word 'boyfriend', and a look passes over her face – is it fear? She immediately begins to backtrack, saying "Oh, it's nothing. Really. Just a little argument over something silly."

"Okay. Sure." I slide into the seat across from her and lean in. "I have a friend who has a whole slew of dating rules and theories, and I'm pretty sure one of them is, if you get into a big fight, never be the one to call first. Whoever calls first is admitting guilt."

A small smile crosses Dee's face. "Thanks, but your friend doesn't know my boyfriend. He would never admit guilt. He's an attorney. Getting into an argument with him is like being cross-examined in a courtroom – even when I know I'm totally right, in the end, he always makes me feel like I'm the one who did something wrong."

"Yikes. He sounds tough. Have you two been together for a long time?"

"About six months – but it feels longer. We met at my work. It was fate. He had some case he was working on and he needed an expert opinion – and someone referred him to me." Dee says dreamily, as she remembers back to the first time she and David met. She seems to already have forgotten how upset she was about a minute ago.

"Oh, wow. That sounds really sweet. So where do you work, then?"

"I work for a company called Code Group . . ." Dee breaks off as her phone pings. She looks down and a smile spreads across her face. "Your friend must be on to something. It's from him. He actually apologized. Look, I have to go, but it was nice meeting you," Dee says as she abruptly stands up and gathers her things. And still looking down at her phone, she rushes out the door.

Using my phone it takes me a few minutes, but I soon find what I'm looking for. It's nice to meet you Diana "Dee" Bartol, expediter. Also known as the permit "issue" with Jane Street.

The streets of the city seem more packed than normal, if that's possible. I can't seem to walk fluidly without being tripped up by someone stopping short or cutting in front of me. Thankfully I am so caught up in my own thoughts, I don't pay anyone any mind. I'm putting one foot in front of the other, sipping my Americano – my surroundings a blur. With the passing of each street sign as I sail past another block, my focus grows stronger. David has a girlfriend. She's an expediter. They were arguing about him lying to her. David knew Chloe and liked to flirt with pretty, young girls. David has a temper. I obviously didn't know David at all – but I think I'm getting to know him all too well now.

Before long I realize I'm just about through Chelsea and almost in Tribeca. I made a plan this morning before David sidetracked me, and I'm going to stick to it. I need to speak with the new owners of the Tribeca Park Building apartment that Josh renovated. Hopefully I can decipher the exact partnership that Josh and Chloe had. Something has not been adding up.

I make a turn and head west toward the Hudson River. And there, looming in front of me is the Merkin House. I start to feel nauseous and my heart aches. I take a deep breath, trying not to think of the feel of Ryker's hand on my lower back, and I walk on.

The lobby of the Tribeca Park Building is practically empty. I was hoping for a bustle of people that would allow me to slip over to the elevators unnoticed. That is not going to happen. If only Tessa were here with me, she can charm her way into anywhere.

Casually strolling up to the front desk, I flash my biggest smile at the doorman. He looks up from his magazine, his eyes at half-staff, and asks, "Can I help you?" with as little enthusiasm as humanly possible.

"Hi there! I was here last week meeting with a contractor who recently finished work on an apartment on the sixth floor. Well, I would love the chance to speak to the new owners of that apartment. You see, before I hire the same contractor, I'd like to see what they thought of him. You know what I mean? It's just such a big decision and everything." The doorman just looks at me, so I keep rambling on. "You would really be helping me out, big time. I'm just so worried to give this guy all this money before I've spoken to someone else that used him. You know?"

Channeling my negotiations professor in law school who told our class, "Whoever speaks first loses," I tilt my head to the side and smile, waiting. This is awkward.

"I'm not even sure they're home." He finally says, looking bored.

"If they're not home, no problem! But, it can't hurt to try, right?"

He picks up the phone, dials a number and waits. I'm praying someone answers the phone.

"Hello Mrs. Tobin, this is Lenny at the door. There's a woman here to see you. She wants to ask you some questions about the contractor who did your apartment?" I wait anxiously for the response. Lenny hangs the phone up and says, "You may go up." And then looks back down at his magazine.

I did it! Tessa would be so proud.

I walk quickly over to the elevators before Lenny can change his mind, completely unaware of the guy in the hoodie sweatshirt watching me from behind a newspaper.

Mrs. Tobin answers the door with a wide smile. "Hello! I'm Janet Tobin, please come in, come in," she says enthusiastically.

I'm guessing Mrs. Tobin is in her late 40s. Her honey colored hair is cut in a bob that frames her face. She has bright hazel eyes and a face full of expression. I like her immediately. I step into the apartment and follow her back into the kitchen. Mrs. Tobin asks if I'd like some coffee or tea.

I point to my to-go coffee cup, and say, "I just grabbed a cup on the way down here, but thank you."

"Silly me!" Mrs. Tobin says and laughs at herself. "I don't know how I didn't see that, you'll have to forgive me. With the renovation and moving – it's been a little crazy around here. Or,

I've been a little crazy around here. I'm going to make myself a cup of coffee, if you don't mind," she says.

"Not at all. It's that time of day, isn't it?"

"It sure is," Mrs. Tobin says. "So let's get right down to it. You are considering using Josh Mesa to do the construction on your home?" she asks me as she pours coffee into a big white mug.

"Yes, I am. It's just such a big decision. I thought I would feel better speaking with someone else who used him as well. So thank you for your time today. How did you like Mr. Mesa?" I'm not wasting any time.

"It was a great experience. He is a perfectionist and very serious about his job. One of the few contractors I've come across who actually shows up on time, and does what he says he's going to do, when he says he's going to do it."

"Did you have an opportunity to meet with his team? His carpenter, or designer?"

"I met the carpenter who did the cabinets in the kitchen for us, and a few other built-ins. Charming guy, his name is John. I think it might be Josh's brother." And then Mrs. Tobin pauses and looks down at her coffee. "I'm not even sure how to say this, and I don't want to alarm you in any way."

"I don't scare easy. Please, you can tell me," I reassure her.

"I met Josh's designer, too," Mrs. Tobin says, looking up from her coffee. And although she's looking my way, she's staring right through me. Her green and yellow-specked eyes glaze over as she remembers. "The designer, her name was Chloe, and she was a doll. A young blonde thing, full of energy."

"I'm not sure if you saw the article in the paper," Mrs. Tobin seems to have snapped out of the spell she was under. She shifts her weight and sets her coffee mug down on the counter. "There was a body found in a building down in the Village . . . It was Chloe's body," she says, looking for my shocked response, which I give her.

"Oh my! How horrible! I did see that in the paper. I can't believe that woman was the designer that helped you with your home! Are you okay?" I feign surprise, but am sincerely concerned. I can tell Mrs. Tobin is taking Chloe's death hard.

"It is just so awful - and scary. If you had known her you would understand. She was so full of life. We worked closely together for months getting everything perfect for this place – I really can't believe she's gone. Who would do this to such a sweet girl? I don't understand what's happening in our world today. I'm praying the police quickly catch whoever did this," Mrs. Tobin's voice shakes with emotion. She gently dabs her eyes with her fingers, pushing the tears away, and takes a deep breath. "Whew, I apologize. This is just all still new," she says.

"Please don't apologize. I completely understand. You have been very helpful and I can go and let you get back to your day. I did have just one more question, if you don't mind?" I ask.

Mrs. Tobin appears to have pulled herself back together. That's what people do after a death – you have to push the pain and grief deep down so it can't bubble to the surface at any moment. You have to move forward. Life goes on, sometimes surprisingly.

"Of course, what else would you like to know?" Mrs. Tobin says with a sad smile.

"Would you mind showing me the Certificate of Completion you received when the work was finished?" I just keep thinking about all those "Happy Clients" on Chloe's website, holding up their Certificates with pride.

"Certificate of Completion?" Mrs. Tobin says, looking confused.

"Yes, the certificate you get after the city does the walk-through and approves the work. You did receive one of those, right?"

"Hmmm, I don't think we did. In fact, I'm sure we didn't. Maybe that's something that Josh keeps? I'll have to ask him."

"You did have a work permit, right?"

"Well yes, of course. It was hung up in plain sight the whole time the work was being done."

"You don't still have the permit, do you?" I ask hopefully.

"No, I'm afraid I don't," says Mrs. Tobin.

I know at this moment that something isn't right. Everyone that does major construction work receives a Certificate of Completion at the end of the project. Why does it seem like none of Josh's clients receive this? It's the follow up to the work permit, and he definitely gets the permit.

I chat with Mrs. Tobin politely for a few more minutes, trying to hide the fact that I'm anxious to get out of there. But Mrs. Tobin wants to show me all around the apartment. I understand that she's excited, and I'm thankful that she took the time to see me, so I follow her from room to room as she points out all the details, changes, and design decisions.

At some point I ask Mrs. Tobin if I can use the ladies room. I feel this might be a good segue to my escape. She insists I use the master bath so that I can admire the tile work. It's' the only room we have yet to swoon over.

Once I open the bathroom door, I stop short. That familiar cold, thick air surrounds me. I can smell the pungent sweet scent. I look on the beautiful marble countertop, and there it is: a Jo Malone Peony and Blush Suede $450 candle. It's not lit, but that smell still permeates the room. Seeing the candle on the counter, I don't feel like my legs are going to give out, but I can't move. I can't go any further into the bathroom. It's as if there is an invisible wall in front of me, shielding me from the pain that hides within these bathroom walls. I take a few deep breaths, and slowly back away from the door.

Walking back out to the kitchen, I thank Mrs. Tobin for seeing me. Pretending to have a work meeting I forgot about, I explain that I must get going. I need to get out of this apartment immediately.

Once outside in the crisp autumn air I take a few more deep breaths and decide to walk. I'm not even sure where I'm going, but I know that keeping my body moving is helping me think. And I sure have a lot to sort through. I head east, happy to get lost in the throngs of people moving about on the sidewalk.

Obviously, the candle was a favorite of Chloe's, and she must have used it in many of the homes she designed and staged. I have confirmed the candle is at Ryker's and the Tobin's. I wonder if it is in David's office? I wish I had thought to look.

The lack of a Certificate of Completion letter at the Tobin's – that's strange. Does Josh not find it important for his client's to see the letter? I know he gets the permit; he got one for Jane Street. I never really took notice, but I wonder if the permit is posted in the window at Jane Street – I think it's supposed to be. Maybe I should ask some of Josh's other past clients if they received Certificates of Completion. That will be my next step.

I will also research work permits in the city. And then I should stop into Jane Street to check out our permit. Maybe I'll find some answers there; although, the thought of going back to Jane Street makes me shudder with dread. Unfortunately, there are not many happy memories from that building at this point. Maybe I'll wait until tomorrow morning - going at night might be too creepy.

Up ahead of me a bar has their cellar door open; the wooden stairs down to their storage area are exposed. A couple of guys are going in and out carrying cases of vodka and gin down the stairs. Completely caught up in my own thoughts, I don't notice the man who has been following me since I left the Tribeca Park Building. As I'm coming up next to the open cellar, the man speeds up, and in a flash he's right next to me. He then lowers his shoulder and gives me a violent push. I am so caught off guard, it's as if I've just been hit from the side by a bus. With nothing to grab onto, there's no way to stop my body from falling into the open cellar. Twisting in mid-air, I'm now heading head first down a steep flight of stairs. I put my arms out in front of me, hoping my hands will break my fall, and brace myself for impact.

As I'm flying down the stairs, one of the workers who was unloading the truck is walking up the stairs. His eyes get big as he sees me coming down, and he freezes in shock. Thankfully for me, hitting this big guy's chest is a lot softer than hitting the concrete floor of the basement. I knock the poor guy flat on his back and land completely on top of him. The side of my face hits the stair railing and I'm seeing stars. One of my arms gets caught under the big guy's weight and pain shoots up my arm. The two of us just stop and look at each other for a minute, a real intimate position to be in for two people who have never met each other.

I try to roll off him, but my arm is stuck. He lifts his one shoulder so I can pull my arm out. I wince in pain as I slowly free my arm from under his weight, and then I just roll over onto my back and stare up at the ceiling.

"Ma'am, are you alright?" The guy asks me.

"Yes, I'm okay. Are you okay? I'm so sorry, I don't know what happened." As I'm talking, I realize I'm shaking. If I cry right now I'll be so mad at myself.

Then I hear footsteps rushing down the wooden steps and I see two men looking down at our contorted bodies sprawled on the basement floor. One guy is young and has on a backward baseball hat, and the other is a little older with a scruffy beard and a wrinkled striped button down shirt.

"Holy shit, are you two okay?! That was crazy!" Backward hat guy says, not giving us time to respond. "I mean, that guy just walked right up next to you and pushed you down a flight of stairs. Did you know him?"

"Wait, what?" I say. "What guy? I thought someone just bumped into me . . ." I can't even continue talking. I realize this young guy is right. Someone just threw me down a flight of stairs, and if I hadn't landed on this thick guy, I could have been seriously hurt, at best.

"Oh, it was definitely on purpose. It was like a hockey check, only not into a wall," Backward Hat just can't stop talking.

This is the most exciting thing that has ever happened to him while at work.

"Kev, be quiet," scruffy beard says to Backward Hat. "Ma'am, are you okay? That was quite a fall."

"Yeah, I think I'm okay," I say, still in shock. "My wrist hurts."

"Okay, I already called an ambulance - just don't move. Rocco, are you alright?" Scruffy beard asks the guy I tackled.

"Yeah, I'm good. Definitely didn't see that one coming," he says as he sits up.

The sound of sirens getting gradually louder and louder fills the basement. A swirling flash of red and yellow lights illuminates the stairwell. A police officer and an EMT come rushing down the stairs. Things are getting really tight down here. It's a small space for Rocco, Kevin, scruffy beard, a police officer, an EMT and me. I sit up and start to feel panicky, like there's no air.

Thankfully, Rocco stands up, and says he'll wait outside. Scruffy beard tells Kevin to leave. Scruffy beard is apparently the owner of the bar, and he explains to the officer everything that happened. Although I'm listening to what the officer and the EMT are asking me, and I'm answering their questions, mentally I am on another planet. All I keep thinking is that someone did this on purpose. Someone tried to hurt me? Kill me?

"Verity? Verity, are you still with us?" The EMT is asking me.

"Yes. I'm here," I whisper.

"Well, Verity, you've got some bumps and bruises, but the good news is, I don't think you broke your wrist. It looks like a nasty sprain. I'm going to wrap it for you, and give you some ibuprofen for the swelling and pain. Do your best to rest it for the next 48 hours if possible. And keep some ice on that cheek, you're going to have quite a bruise.

I just nod my head.

And then the police officer, Officer Camden, is back and a million questions are being thrown at me: *Did you see the man that pushed you? Can you remember what he was wearing? Can you think of anyone who would want to hurt you? Has anything strange happened lately?*

I'm in such a state, that this last question almost makes me laugh - like the delirious laugh of a crazy woman. Anything strange? How about being haunted by the ghost of a girl, and then finding the body of that same girl buried in a wall? Oh, and my friends and business associates are suspects in the murder. Heck, maybe I'm a suspect too. And tonight someone threw me down a flight of stairs hoping to kill me. So yeah, a few strange things have been happening lately.

Out loud I just answer "no" to all his questions. And for the most part, it's the truth. I didn't see the person who pushed me, not even his clothes. I have no idea who would want to hurt me, besides Chloe's murderer, and I don't know who that is. And, to avoid being thrown in the loony bin, I refrain from telling the officer the absurd details of my life right now.

"Is there someone you can call to come get you? Maybe someone who can stay with you tonight? You really shouldn't be alone," Officer Camden looks concerned. He thinks I might be in danger. Am I in danger?

There's only one person I want to be with tonight. And despite the fear I have of putting them in danger, I know I can't be alone. So, I suck up my pride, put my guilt aside, and make the call.

Sitting on the curb I wait while the police and ambulance wrap things up. I hold an ice pack against my face with my right hand, since my left wrist is wrapped in a bandage. I shiver, and I don't know if it's because I'm holding ice and it's cold outside, or if it's my body's response to the trauma. Officer Camden is staying busy, but I know he's waiting until someone comes to meet me and take me home. About twenty minutes later a cab comes screeching to a halt in front of the bar. The door swings open and I see the blonde curls before I see her face. Tessa jumps out of the cab, and looks around frantically. Our eyes meet, and she sprints toward me.

"Oh my god, Verity," she says as she bends down and grabs me in a huge hug. I bury my banged up face into her hair, so relieved to have her here.

"Are you okay?" Her voice sounds muffled, since I'm lost in her wild mane. I nod my head without moving away from her.

"Let's go home."

I lean back and wipe the tears from my eyes. Tessa is staring at me, and I know she's thinking: "Oh no, Verity never cries. This is bad."

But she doesn't say anything. She just puts my left arm around her neck, grabs me around the waist with her right arm and hoists us both up to standing. Officer Camden sees us and walks over.

"Well, Ms. Townsend, I'm glad you've got someone to get you home. I have to admit, I was hoping it would be someone about 6'5", maybe with a black belt.

"I can take care of her," Tessa says defensively.

"We'll be fine. We're tougher than we look," I reassure him.

Tessa helps me hobble over to the waiting cab, and I collapse in the seat. She slides in next to me and gives the driver my address. I doze off during the drive up town, my head leaning on Tessa's shoulder. Even though I know she's dying to ask me a million questions, she lets me rest. I can't remember ever being so exhausted.

Tessa gently shakes me awake and I'm completely disoriented. My face must show as much, because Tessa says, "V, we're home. Let's go." I slide out of the cab and somehow make it up the front steps. Tessa has my purse and is routing around for my keys. What would I do without her? The thought brings more tears to my eyes, but thankfully Tessa is too busy unlocking the door to notice. Me, this emotional, that would really freak her out.

Once inside, Tessa locks the door behind us and sets the alarm. We walk through the kitchen and into the living room, turning on lights as we go. Tessa walks over to the fireplace and points at it – her way of asking me if I'd like it on. I nod. I can't seem to shake the chill I've had since the fall. I plop myself on my couch, pull off my boots and throw them on the floor, and wrap a blanket around my shoulders. Tessa flips the switch to turn on the fireplace, and then walks directly over to the wine rack. She pulls a bottle of Cabernet out of the rack, opens it and pours two giant glasses of wine. She then sits next to me on the couch, hands me a glass and says, "Okay. What the hell just happened?"

I take a long sip of my wine. I start with last night at Ryker's, his beautiful apartment, the food, the wine – the candle. I tell her about David and Mrs. Tobin and the Certificate of Completion. And then, I tell her about tonight. The unknown man body-checking me down an open cellar door and down a flight of stairs. While I talk, I absentmindedly touch my bandaged wrist.

Tessa stays quiet through most of my ramblings, asking almost no questions, just letting me get it all out. When I'm finally done I look over at her, waiting for a response. Without saying a word, she walks back over to the bar cart, refills her wine glass, walks back over to the couch and says, "You need to call Detective O'Donnell." As I begin to disagree, she stops me short. "This has gone too far, Verity. Obviously, the killer knows you are looking into things and he wants you out of the picture. And by that I mean - dead. He wants you dead. You need police protection, or you need to leave the city for a little bit - or maybe both. You know you can stay with my parents in Albany. They would love to see you," she goes on getting excited about the idea. I stop her mid-sentence, "Tess, I'm not leaving town. Don't you see? What happened tonight means I'm close. I'm on to something. The killer thinks I'm going to find out who he is, and guess what, he's right."

"Verity, you are not a detective. You don't have back up to call when this nut job discovers you didn't die tonight, and he needs to come back and finish the job. You don't own a gun, nor are you trained in jujitsu. If you're not going to leave town, then you have to call Detective O'Donnell and tell him what you've discovered. Maybe together with what he's found out, you two can figure it out faster," Tessa is trying to sound hopeful.

"The problem is, I don't have any evidence. Everything I've 'found' either a ghost told me in a dream or is based off my gut feelings and intuition. No sane detective is going to listen to me."

"Well, then you call him and you tell him what happened to you tonight. That should be enough for him. And then he can get you a bodyguard or whatever they do."

When I start to shake my head with a rebuttal, Tessa cuts me off, "Nope, this is non-negotiable. You are calling Detective O'Donnell tomorrow and you are going to tell him someone tried to kill you tonight. End of story."

I look at Tessa, see her determined face and know that she's right. That and because I don't want her to worry, I agree, "Okay. I'll call the detective tomorrow." Tessa smiles. "Thank you. I feel better now."

"Good. But now, I have to go to bed. I don't think my eyes will stay open anymore," I tell her. And I mean it, my whole body has started to ache as the adrenaline and medicine wears off. My face hurts, and my wrist hurts and I just want to crawl into a ball and sleep for days.

Up in my room, I put on some flannel pajamas, swallow a few more ibuprofens and snuggle under the covers. My soft bed envelops me in warm hug, and I'm asleep in minutes.

Chapter 23

Whoa! She did not see that coming! She must weigh next to nothing the way she flew down that open cellar. I wish I could have seen her face as she met her end, but desperate times call for desperate measures. I had to get out of there. She was getting too close - talking to Chloe's roommate, and then talking to the Tobin's. What could she possibly have been asking them anyway? Well, I no longer need to worry about that. I saw that open cellar door up ahead, the thought came to me, and I acted. Boom. That's the sign of a leader. I'm someone that can act and react - someone who can execute a plan, and also improvise. It really could not have worked out better. There's no way anyone was paying attention to me, or got a good look at me. It happened so fast; she literally didn't know what hit her.

All I need to do now is go back to Jane Street and tie up a few loose ends. I would have done that already if not for the constant swarm of police over there. I'll try again tomorrow. And then I can put this whole thing behind me, and continue to conquer Manhattan.

Chapter 24

Waking up, I think it's a normal morning until I try to move and my body feels like a Mack truck hit it. Too quickly, the details from last night come flashing back to me, making me want to roll over and go back to sleep. I turn onto my side and see a mop of blonde curls next to me. Tessa. She must have slept in here with me last night. Maybe that's why I had such a good night sleep.

Being careful not to wake her, I slip my feet into my fuzzy slippers and slink downstairs. I put on a pot of coffee and sit in my favorite morning spot – my gray wingback chair. With my coffee mug in hand I stare out the window, watching the world wake up. Lost in thought, I don't realize Tessa has come downstairs until I hear her messing around in the cabinets looking for a coffee mug.

"I put one right next to the coffee maker for you," I tell her. I smile as she rolls her eyes at herself.

"Ugh, thank you. You know me, I am *so* not a morning person," Tessa tells me for the thousandth time.

"You don't say?" I tease her. "But seriously, how'd you sleep?"

"I slept fine. I hope you don't mind that I climbed in bed with you. I wanted to be sure I knew where you were, and I also didn't want to be alone either. You know, the whole a-murderer-is-after-you thing."

"Oh, yeah. That thing," I say.

"Ouch, that's quite a bruise on your cheek," Tessa says as she walks over to me and sits down on the couch. I gently rub my fingers over my tender cheek, "Yeah, I don't know how I'm going to hide this. I may need your makeup skills today," I tell her.

"Why, where are you going?" Tessa asks. "I was hoping you'd stay locked up in your castle all day like a Princess hiding from an evil witch."

"Well, I have a few things I want to check out - nothing to worry about," I reassure her.

Tessa's phone goes off and she checks it. "Ugh, I have to go in to work today. I'm so sorry. I have this big photo shoot coming up and they have all the collaborators coming to meet on location," Tessa explains, and I know she feels guilty, which is ridiculous. "I know the timing of this isn't great, but I have been so excited about this project in particular. The actual photo shoot won't be for a few months, but get this, I get to work with Alexandra Pickoski!"

"Am I supposed to know who that is?

"Yes! She's only the most amazing fashion photographer in the world. And I'm going to get to work with her! And there's more," Tessa is bubbling over at this point, "the shoot is taking place at the Dakota Building!"

Tessa cannot contain her excitement. This is obviously very important to her.

"The place where Lennon was shot? That is so exciting! And you get to help design the set?" I ask her.

"Yes, I'm second lead on this one, which is amazing. And we are going to pitch a few ideas to the whole group today. I hope to bring in elements of the paranormal, with ghostly pale women in white flowing dresses. You know, because the place is known to be haunted. If it weren't such a big deal, you know I would totally skip today. I wish I didn't have to leave you here alone." Tessa says, sounding worried.

"Don't be silly! Please, do what you need to do for work. I'm going to be mostly laying low today anyway. I'm going to run out for one quick errand, and that's it."

"Ok. But don't do anything stupid. I will be back tonight as soon as I can. And, I'm sleeping over again. I like your house better than mine anyway," Tessa smiles. "And do you know what else I like better? Your closet. I'm sorry to say, I'm going to have to borrow something to wear to work today. Darn!" Tessa says sarcastically.

"Of course. Go to town." Tessa jumps up and hustles upstairs to my closet. "So much for not being a morning person," I yell after her.

I'm not quite ready to separate myself from this chair, but I push myself to standing and limp over to re-fill my coffee. With my fresh cup of coffee, my phone and my laptop, I hobble back over to the gray wingback and settle in.

My phone shows a missed call from Ryker. Only one, maybe he's giving up. I don't know how that makes me feel – relieved or devastated? There is also a missed call from Evelyn.

In speaking with Evelyn, I downplay everything that has happened. I tell her I had a bad fall and have a sprained wrist. She is so worried, I can't even imagine how she'd react if she knew the truth. If Evelyn ever thought I was in danger, she would insist on coming over today, and I really just want to be alone. I tell her I'm feeling fine, just tired and achy and explain I'm going to work from home today. She tells me to rest and not worry about a thing. If only not worrying were an option.

Evelyn then brings up David, and is going on and on about how he's doing. She explains that no charges have been brought against him, but Detective O'Donnell brought him in and questioned him for hours. She says David seems most angry about how he's being treated by the authorities.

"David seems to have quite the temper," I say.

"He can. But that's partly what makes him so good at his job." Evelyn says, and I can hear her getting defensive. I think I'll wait until I have some more information about David and Chloe before I tell Evelyn what I know about him. But, that conversation will have to happen at some point.

Evelyn and I talk for a few more minutes and then I promise to check in again with her later today. I hang up and immediately begin to check my emails. While I'm working, Tessa comes down dancing through my kitchen flaunting a floral dress with a blazer, and ankle boots. I would never have put these three pieces of clothing together, but on Tessa they look artsy and eclectic.

"You look great!" I tell her. "Did you have fun?"

"I did have fun. I loved turning your tunic top into a dress! And it got me thinking – if you're going to have some psycho killer after you, I might have to stay here for a loooong time. I want you to know that I am totally cool with that. I will sleep here, and get dressed here for as many days or weeks as needed. I will make that sacrifice for you."

"Wow. You are such a good friend. What would I ever do without you?" And then we're both laughing.

"However, I may need to stop and get some real food for that giant, empty refrigerator," she says on her way out.

I ignore her comment, and call after her, "Have a great day, dear."

Once Tessa is gone, I finish responding to my work emails, and then get to what I've been waiting to do since last night. I start by searching for a photo of what a work permit looks like. I find a picture of one, but on the computer it just looks like a black and white piece of paper, nothing special. However, I then find an article about the Quick Response code, or QR code, as they are more commonly known, that are now mandatory on permits. New Yorkers can scan the code and learn details about ongoing projects, read any complaints and or violations related to the location, or click on a link to make a complaint of their own. I am so excited about this, I jump up from my chair. Unfortunately, I am quickly reminded that I was thrown down a flight of stairs yesterday, as pain shoots up my arm, my back, and my side. But I don't care, this is exactly what I needed, I just know it.

The air around me suddenly goes still. The flames from the fire abruptly go out, as if someone flipped the switch off. And then, the screen on my laptop goes black. Staring at the screen, goosebumps form on my arms and a chill comes over my body. Images start flashing up on the screen. One, then another, and another - they're coming too fast for me to see what they are. The air around me turns ice cold, my hair stands on end and I slowly put the computer down on the coffee table. Chloe. Now the laptop isn't flashing, but instead, fifty different browser windows are open all to the same webpage. When the screen finally goes still, I cautiously move closer to see what Chloe is trying to show me.

Elma Sands. It's an article about the Elma Sands murder. Although I feel like I already know the story, I read the article looking for some clue as to why that murder would be important to Chloe. Elma was drowned. Her lover, Eli Weeks, was accused of the murder. Ezra Weeks hires Hamilton and Burr to defend Eli. And Eli gets acquitted. Some people were angry - they thought Eli was guilty.

After my first read-through of the article, nothing stands out to me that could help with solving Chloe's murder. I read it again. Maybe that's why she opened the page fifty times - it might take me that long to figure it out. What do the two cases have in common? Elma and Chloe were both drowned. Is Chloe trying to say her lover did it? Is Johnny guilty? I think of the heartbroken man I saw sitting across from me at the bar, and I have a really hard time believing that. But I need to keep an open mind.

I skim to re-read all the parts about Eli. He was a carpenter living in the same boarding house as Elma. Huh, I didn't know Eli was a carpenter. And Ezra was a successful builder who built the Hamilton Grange Mansion for Alexander Hamilton. So Ezra was a builder and Eli was a carpenter . . .

Chapter 25

I'm racing down to the Village in a cab that just can't seem to go fast enough. Between the coffee and the adrenaline my right leg won't stop bouncing. I open the *NY Post* app on my phone, thinking I'll read the paper to distract myself from the frustrating traffic. My heart stops, and I let out a gasp as I read today's headline:

MARRIED MAN HAVING AFFAIR WITH MURDERED GIRL

Johnny. I click on the headline to read the whole article:

John Mesa is being questioned in the murder of young Chloe Kingston. The two were having a secret affair, and according to Chloe's roommate, Chloe was pressuring Johnny to leave his wife, Melissa Mesa. Johnny, as he's known to friends, along with being a talented carpenter, also has the reputation of being quite popular with women.

The article goes on to give a quick summary of Chloe and her murder. It explains what Chloe did for a living, and where she was found (of course they had to mention the building was owned by CFF, ugh). It also notes that a former client of hers, David Cohen, was questioned and released yesterday with no charges filed against him. Well, at least the media is no longer focused on David. Actually, maybe I should connect Johnny and David. It sounds like Johnny might need a good defense attorney.

Finally, the cab is pulling up to Jane Street. Thankfully I don't see any police cars still lingering around, so I should be able to get in and out undisturbed. I have my key ready, and I run up the front steps. It takes me a minute of wiggling the key around in the old sticky lock, but I finally get it unlocked. Pushing aside a piece of the yellow caution tape, I step into Jane Street. The building is dark, cold and dusty. With every move my footsteps echo through the halls, leaving me feeling on edge. I walk straight over to the front window where the building permit is displayed, and take the permit down. As far as I can tell it looks exactly like the photos I saw online. If I don't find any answers with this permit, I'll be back to square one. The only evidence I'll have that one or both of the Mesa brothers are responsible for Chloe's death, will have come from supernatural sources. I'm pretty sure ghosts don't make reliable witnesses.

I quickly realize I have no idea how to use the QR, so I have to do an Internet search on my phone to figure it out. I need to download a barcode scanner app. My shaky fingers keep clicking on the wrong links and letters, but finally I have the barcode scanner app downloaded. Clicking on the app, I then hold my phone so that the camera is directly over the barcode on the permit. Holding my breath, I anxiously await the outcome – and nothing happens. Nothing. I try again and this time, the app displays a message that says "Invalid Barcode." Frustrated, I want to throw my phone across the room. And then it hits me. The barcode doesn't work, because the barcode is invalid. It's a fake.

Suddenly, a sharp pain shoots through the back of my head, disrupting my thoughts and hurling my body forward.

Down on all fours, I shake my head in an attempt to clear my vision. I turn my head to look behind me and see the outline of a tall, dark haired man. Although his face is blurry, I know who it is.

"Hi Josh." My voice comes out scratchy.

"Verity. It's so nice to see you again," Josh says with dark sarcasm. "I didn't think I'd ever be seeing you again after last night, but you have proven much more resilient than I was giving you credit for. Now I know better."

Turning around, I sit on the floor facing him. I lean back, putting all my weight on my good wrist, and do my best to appear in control. My head is throbbing, but I know I need to keep him talking; it might be the only way I get out of here alive.

"The permit's a fake."

Josh starts to clap loudly, a maniacal smile on his face. The echoing claps reverberate through the empty rooms, and definitely don't help my headache.

"Now, aren't you clever. Thankfully, you're a lot more clever than that detective the NYPD put on the job. They're looking in all the wrong places. But not you - not Verity Townsend. Unfortunately for you, your little discovery will die along with you."

As Josh is talking, I slowly ease myself to standing.

"So Chloe figured it out, too. And she made the mistake of telling you first, and not the police."

"Yeah, she figured it out. She threatened to tell my brother, who she was screwing, or go to the police if I didn't stop.

That little slut actually thought she could tell me what to do. She soon realized that wasn't going to happen. I was not going to let some stupid girl ruin everything I have worked for. And I'm not going to let you do that either, Verity."

"Where'd you do it? Where'd you drown her?" I ask him, trying hard to stay standing, and keep him talking. I keep staring at his left hand, which is holding a laptop - Chloe's missing laptop. That's what he hit me with.

"Oh, so you couldn't figure that one out? Oh Verity, I'm disappointed! I thought you were better than that," Josh says, again with a sick smile on his face. He's having fun with this.

"The Tribeca apartment -in the master bathroom." I say, only just putting it together. I was there too that night, meeting Josh for the first time. She must have come over right after I left.

"There you go! Now that's more like it! You two just missed each other, actually. If only I knew things would work out this way – I could've taken care of both of you that night. You know – two birds, one stone. What's with you women? You just can't mind your own business?! She had done all this research and had all this evidence – why did she care? It had nothing to do with her."

As soon as Josh says that last word, I make a run for it. The only direction I can go is through what was the old dining room, I then into the kitchen. I can hear Josh running from the front entry through the hall to enter through the main kitchen door. We enter the kitchen at about the same time. From the corner of my eye I see Josh dive toward me, attempting to tackle me. I move quickly enough that he misses my body, but he gets ahold of my legs and trips me up. I fall hard, putting my hands out in front of me to catch myself, which was a bad idea. As I land on my sprained wrist, the pain is excruciating. That and my pounding head, and I feel like I might black out.

But something is keeping me going: Chloe. I start to scramble around the kitchen floor - feeling all around the tile. It's just like one of the nightmares. I can hear Josh scurry to his feet, and I know he's coming back after me. I keep searching along the tile, not even sure what I'm looking for, my vision still hazy. And then I feel the laptop smack the back of my head again, and I fall flat, splayed out on the tile. Josh's heavy breathing pulsing in my ears. Something, or someone, takes my good arm and moves it around until I feel my hand land on something hard and metal. A wrench.

An unearthly strength consumes my body as I grab ahold of the wrench and spin around with all my might. I swing the wrench in the direction of the shadowy figure and feel the thick thud as I make contact. I hear Josh fall to the floor, his body smacking against the tile.

It might be a dream, but I am now aware of a bright ball of light in front of my eyes. The light is being pulled, summoned, further and further away. Translucent layers of light surround me, and I feel love, security and the presence of nurturing thoughts. All these feelings I have felt before, many years ago. The soft sound of musical tranquility fills my ears – twinkling bells and strings. Bye, Chloe. May your soul Rest In Peace.

Chapter 26

The sounds of beeping machines and the smell of bleach assault my senses. I attempt to crack my eyes open, but the stream of light is so bright, I quickly shut them tight again. I tilt my head the slightest bit, and intense pain throbs behind my eyes.

"Verity," a woman's voice whispers. "Verity, don't try and move sweetheart."

"Where am I?" I ask the voice, still unable to open my eyes.

"You're at the hospital, honey," the now familiar voice says.

"Evelyn?" I ask, my eyes fluttering. I try and sit up a little, but my head feels like it weighs two hundred pounds.

"Oh, don't try and sit up. I wish I knew how to work this darn bed. Wait one minute, I just called for the nurse."

A nurse rushes in, and pushes a button that rotates the bed to a sitting position. I am now sitting up, but thankfully don't have to lift my head on my own - it can stay resting on the pillow.

"Ms. Townsend, it's nice to have you back with us. How are you feeling?" The nurse asks me.

"Ouch," is all I can say. I reach my hand up to touch my aching head, and feel the bandage. My bad wrist now has a cast on it; I'm assuming it's broken for sure this time. I am a wreck.

Footsteps and voices coming from the hall disrupt my injury inventory. Tessa, Mitchell, and Ryker enter the room, and all three stop dead in their tracks when they see me sitting up.

Tessa is the first to come back to life. She runs over to me, engulfing me in a giant bear hug. It hurts everywhere, but I let her do it.

"Thank God you're okay," Tessa whispers in my ear.

Mitchell and Ryker slowly walk over to the bed but stand back far enough to give Tessa and me some space. Mitchell is smiling warmly at me. Ryker looks pale and ... worried.

"Ouch, Tessa," I say, realizing if I don't say something she may never let go of me.

"Whoops, sorry," Tessa says with a nervous giggle, as she finally releases me from her grasp.

"What happened?" I ask, looking at all of them.

"We were hoping you'd tell us," Mitchell says.

"I found you ... at Jane Street," Ryker says, his eyes big and dark. "Well, Detective O'Donnell and I found you. You were lying on the floor in the kitchen. I thought you were ... You were lying next to Josh Mesa. The two of you, completely knocked out, laying next to each other."

"Is Josh ..."

"He's here. He's here in the hospital. He's still alive, unfortunately." Anger flashes in Ryker's eyes like I've never seen before.

It all comes rushing back to me. "Chloe. The laptop. Where's the laptop? And the permit - the permit's fake." I start to feel frantic and panicky. I need go, to get up, to do something.

Evelyn and Tessa rush to my side, gently petting me, and telling me to calm down in soft voices. But I can't calm down. Someone needs to get Josh before he gets away.

"Can I have a minute with Ms. Townsend, please?" A booming voice interrupts my panicked rambling, and the room goes completely quiet. I follow the voice and see Detective O'Donnell's hulking frame in the doorway.

"I'm not sure this is a good time," Evelyn says firmly.

"It won't take long," the Detective says as he walks up to the bed.

"It's okay. I'm okay." I tell everyone staring at me. Reluctantly, they slowly file out of the room.

"How are you feeling, Ms. Townsend?" Detective O'Donnell asks me, as he pulls up a seat next to the bed.

"I've been better."

"I would think so. You're lucky to be alive. Now, can you tell me why you were at Jane Street today?"

"I was there to look at the work permit in the window."

"Why?"

I feel like I'm in trouble. "I had reason to believe that Josh Mesa was using fraudulent permits at his work sites," I tell him, doing my best to sound professional.

"Well, that was pretty good detective work you did. The only problem with doing your own detective work on a murder case, is that it can get you killed," he scolds me.

I put my head down and look at my hands.

"In the future, Ms. Townsend, if you think you have discovered something that is important to an ongoing case, please call the police. Do not, and I'm going to repeat this so I'm sure you're hearing me, do not try to investigate yourself."

"Yes, sir," I say quietly. And then I look up and ask, "How did you know I was at Jane Street?"

"We had Josh Mesa under surveillance."

"Wait, why did you have him under surveillance?"

"In Chloe's room we found a list of apartments. It didn't take us long to figure out they were all spaces Josh had worked on. And we knew she had these specific places printed out and protected in a folder for a reason."

I nod my head.

"Anyway, as I was saying before I was interrupted. We watched him go inside and were hoping he was going in to find Chloe's laptop and phone, which he was. He had hidden the laptop and phone in the basement of Jane Street – I'm pretty sure he was in panic mode. He drowned Chloe in an apartment he had been renovating, and then didn't know what to do with her body. So, knowing Jane Street would be empty – we think on Friday afternoon, he hid her body and her things there. He couldn't have planned to leave her there for a long period of time, or the body would start to smell. And trust me, that is a smell you would not be able to ignore. So he puts her in the wall, temporarily, seals it up, and hides her laptop and phone in the utility room in the basement. When he went back to get her things today, I don't know who was more surprised you were in there – Josh or us."

"Then how was Ryker there too?" I ask, trying to piece it all together.

"Your curly haired friend called Mr. Rensselaer and told him what happened to you last night. She was worried with you being home alone all day. And can I just stop and say, if someone ever tries to kill you again, please call the police and let them know," he says, exasperated.

I nod my head.

"Anyway," the Detective continues, "Mr. Rensselaer went to your house to check up on you, saw you getting into a cab and tried to follow you. He lost you in traffic on the way downtown, but thought you were headed to the Village. He checked Jane Street to see if you were there. When he pulled up, we, the police that is, were just pulling up as well. We all went in together. But it was Mr. Rensselaer who found you first. I thought he was going to pass out right there next to you, poor guy."

My face turns red with a heat coming from deep inside my body. For an instant, I no longer feel any pain, just a euphoric fluttering low in my belly.

"Ms. Townsend, you must be one of the luckiest women I've ever met. You survived two attempts on your life, stayed conscious through some painful head trauma, and knocked out a guy twice your size. But, what makes you the luckiest are the people you have in your life who obviously care for you deeply."

Detective O'Donnell then heaves himself up to standing. "There's one more person who would like a word with you, if you're up for it."

Shifting my eyes towards the door, I see nothing but Detective O'Donnell's wide body blocking my line of vision. Once I have a clear view, who is left standing there looking at me with red-rimmed eyes, but Johnny Mesa. At first glance, I don't even recognize him – he stands with his shoulders slumped and his hands thrust in the pockets of a gray hooded sweatshirt. He hasn't shaved in days. Greasy, tangled hair hangs over his eyes, which look empty and lost. It's a far cry from the charismatic guy I met a week ago.

"Can I come in?" He asks me quietly, obviously unsure about my answer.

I nod my head.

He walks in slowly, head down, feet barely lifting off the ground.

"How are you feeling?" He asks, daring to look me in the eyes.

"I'll live. You look awful."

Johnny lets a sad laugh escape. "You don't look so hot yourself."

We look at each other, and a whole conversation takes place within our stare.

"I don't know what to say."

"There's nothing for you to say. I understand," I try to unburden him from the guilt and responsibility obviously crushing him from the inside out.

"And here I thought I was the family delinquent."

"Trust me. You are," I say with a teasing smile.

"Thank you, Verity. And please, if you ever need anything . . ."

I nod my head, "Bye, Johnny. Take care of yourself."

Exhausted and weak, I doze for an unknown period of time. When I awake it feels late. The blinds are closed, and a green light from the machines I'm hooked up to gives the room an eerie glow. The beeping of the machines is steady like a heartbeat. Glancing around the room I'm surprised to see I'm not alone. Ryker is sleeping in a most uncomfortable looking position on a tiny chair. I take the opportunity to stare openly at him. His long legs are stretched out in front of him, and crossed at the ankles, with his arms folded across his chest. He looks peaceful.

As if he can sense my staring, his eyes flutter open. Looking over at me and seeing me awake, he pops up to a sitting position.

"Verity, how are you feeling? Can I get you anything?" He asks, walking over to me.

"Maybe some water?" My voice comes out hoarse.

Ryker busies himself pouring water into a plastic cup. "

What time is it? Why are you still here? You should go home and get some sleep."

"It's probably around midnight - you've been sleeping most of the day. I told everyone else to go home and sleep for a few hours, and that I would hold down the fort here in case you woke up. I had to fight to be the one to stay, but you know me, I always win." And there's that smile I could stare at forever.

I take a sip of the cold water, and it feels so good on my parched throat.

"Ryker, I really need to apologize to you for the other night. It's kind of a strange thing that happened, and if I explained it to you, then you might think I'm completely insane. But the candle . . ."

"Verity," Ryker interrupts me, "You don't need to explain anything to me. Obviously, I now realize you have been going through some pretty crazy stuff. And the candle - I was baffled when you said that. I was up all that night trying to figure out what you were talking about. When I went into that hall bathroom the next day, I saw the candle on the counter and realized where I got it. It was part of a gift basket Chloe sent me after she did that work for me – as a thank you. I had completely forgotten about it."

"I'm so sorry. I knew that candle was linked to Chloe and . . ."

"Please, don't worry about it. I just wish you had confided in me sooner about everything going on. I might've been able to help."

"I guess I'm not used to going to people with my problems. I've pretty much handled things on my own for as long as I can remember."

"About that," Ryker says, "I've got something for you."

Ryker walks back to the tiny chair he was folded up on and comes back to my bedside with a stack of papers.

"What's this?"

"I couldn't stop thinking about your family situation," he starts.

I look at him quizzically, waiting to say anything until I know where he's going with this.

"And you know how much I like historical research, right?"

I nod my head.

"Well, I did some research on you. On your family tree," he says as he hands me the papers.

I take the papers in my hand, but I don't know what to say. I'm speechless. I am so touched by the gesture I can barely focus. I do my best to make sense of the names on the family tree. My parents and my grandparents are the only names I have ever known. And to see the names of my great grandparents listed is incredible. As I get further down the line, my jaw drops. In tracing back my family's ancestry, Ryker discovered that I am the great great great great granddaughter of William Bayard.

I look up at him, with my eyes big and my mouth still hanging open, but no words will come to me.

"I know, right." Ryker smiles.

"It's unbelievable that I chose the home for CFF on the piece of property where my ancestors lived over 200 years ago. The connection I always felt at Jane Street, it was real," I say as tears spring to my eyes. This might explain why Chloe came to me for help, I think to myself, but don't dare say out loud. "I don't know how to thank you, Ryker. No one has ever done anything like this for me."

"Well, it was either this or a new pair of Louboutin's."

I roll my eyes at him.

"But seriously, I wanted you to know who your family was. Of course, I had no idea it would turn out this way. That was just pure luck. Want to know another interesting discovery? The Rensselaer family seems to have some ties with the Bayard family going way back. Maybe you were drawn to me by something otherworldly," he says with a smirk.

"Because I love this gift so much, I'm going to let that comment slide. And that is my gift to you," I reply.

"There she is. Verity's back," Ryker says as he takes my hand.

Chapter 27

December

Rushing down Hudson Street, I hug my heavy camel color cashmere coat tight against my body, and bury my chin into my cream wool scarf. The streets are like wind tunnels on this cold, grey day. Although winter has not officially clutched the city in its bone-chilling grasp, it definitely no longer feels like fall.

Thanks to lunch with Ryker, which ran much too long, I'm running late to meet the caterer at Jane Street. And although we were just together, I can't wait to see him again tonight. Tonight is the launch party for the CFF Home. I have spent the past three months working tirelessly to get the renovation done, which of course required a new permit and contractor. But by some miracle we finished enough of it in time to host the launch party before the holidays - which was my goal.

Tonight, after the horrible start to the CFF Home creation, we will finally be able to celebrate helping orphaned children. I have decorated the first floor of the CFF Home with thousands of little lights. The ceilings have little twinkle lights hanging from them, and candles will be lit all over the tables and fireplace mantels. I'm calling the night "The Light of Our Lives," referring to the children, of course. When I saw the space yesterday it looked breathtaking. Invitations went out a month ago, and the response far exceeded our expectations. Although no one will admit to it, there is definitely some type of thrill people expect being somewhere a murder took place. I know a large part of the response was due to a macabre curiosity.

I could remind these people the murder didn't actually take place at the CFF Home; the body was just buried here. But who am I to spoil all their fun. In the end, the goal is to spread the word about what CFF does and raise some much needed funds, of course. As the night goes on, I'm sure there will be plenty of 'selfies' taken in the kitchen with captions like:

"I'm standing where the poor young girl was found murdered #creepy."

It's really interesting how people react to horrific events – it's like staring at a car crash. You don't really want to see the destruction, or see people in pain, but for some reason you can't look away. Tonight I have prepared myself to not take it personally. These people didn't know Chloe, and I'm sure none of them have ever known someone who was murdered. For them it is so far from their reality, it doesn't seem real at all.

As I briskly walk the last block before turning west onto Jane Street, I try to push last night's nightmare out of my mind. I haven't had a nightmare like this one, since, well Chloe. It has been a peaceful few months, which I have enjoyed. However, despite my efforts to forget it, the feeling of falling, and the dark haired woman's terrified brown eyes consumes me.

I get to the steps of 76 Jane Street, and take one last deep breath. It's time to focus on tonight's event. Just then, my phone rings and I see that it's Tessa.

"Hi Tessa, is it important? I'm about to walk into a meeting with . . ."

"V, listen to me," Tessa interrupts me, "I need your help. I don't know what to do. I'm at a photo shoot, and one of the photographers . . . I just found her . . ." Tessa's voice is shaking.

"Tessa, what's wrong. What happened?"

"She's dead, Verity. Alexandra. I found her . . . I found her on the sidewalk. I think someone pushed her."

"What's the address? I'll be right there."

"72nd and Central Park West. The Dakota."

Author's Note

The idea for Jane Street emerged organically from a hobby of reading about ghosts that haunt New York City. Since I was a child I have been intrinsically drawn to the paranormal. I'm fascinated with the idea of tormented souls deciding to stay earthbound after a traumatic death in order to find closure. I have always wished to be someone who can receive messages from those on the other side. However, sadly, no spirits are whispering in my ear, visiting me in my dreams or sending chills up my spine (darn it!). Researching ghosts that are frequently seen around Manhattan, I came upon Alexander Hamilton. His is a tragic story of a great man taken too soon, and I quickly became engrossed in all the facets of his life (this was all before the musical *Hamilton* hit Broadway!). Hamilton led me to the story of poor Elma Sands and her murder. I contemplated writing a historical fiction novel about Elma, but realized I would rather write something current – so I used Elma's story as a parallel to what happened to Chloe Kingston.

The history of Alexander Hamilton dying on Jane Street, and Elma Sands' murder that exists in the book is all historically accurate. 82 Jane Street is an historical landmark, with a plaque stating it to be the former home of William Bayard. It is said to be the place where Alexander Hamilton was brought after the duel, and where he died. Although Alexander Hamilton was brought to William Bayard's house to die, the location is not that of the current day 82 Jane Street, which is on the south side of the street. It actually would have been on the North side of the street closer to where the CFF Home was to be built in my story.

William Bayard was born in Manhattan and died in Westchester, New York, but many of his descendants settled in Albany, New York. This is why I made Albany Verity's hometown. The surname Townsend is found in the actual Bayard family tree, however Verity Townsend is a completely fictional character. Both Alexander Hamilton and William Bayard are buried in the Trinity Church cemetery – definitely worth a visit (at night, if you dare!).

Writing my first mystery novel has been a dream come true. My amazing husband deserves a special thank you for his unconditional support, and constant encouragement. And to my Mom: you got me hooked on mysteries early on with your love for *Murder, She Wrote* and Mary Higgins Clark books. I feel especially lucky you were the first person to read Jane Street, and that you also happen to be the best proofreader and editor a girl could ask for (especially since you work for free!) – thank you.

About the Author

Kate Kasch is a displaced New Englander living in northern New Jersey with her (amazing) husband, and four non-stop children. In order to remain sane, she writes and runs.

Made in the USA
Middletown, DE
10 August 2017